D1355994

Chronicle of a Bounty Hunter

Settlers are now travelling west by wagon trains, the very beginnings of a new life in a new land that is wild, beautiful and free for the ones who make it through. Sharecroppers, under President Lincoln's new law, encourage men and women who are young and strong to tame the huge prairie lands; a land for adventurers; exhilarating, yet brutal. Civilisation struggles for existence there among a plague of human scum.

Jack Hoffmann is a bounty hunter. Survival has made him very special: a legend. In many ways the tall, dark man epitomises what was once the only way for justice to prevail on the Frontier. Instant justice from Peacemaker and scattergun, before the law could reach cow-town, homestead or hovel. His eyes hold a man in fear by his presence alone. These are the chronicles of a loner, Jack Hoffmann; stories of instant justice spread evenly amongst the most degenerate hoodlums the West ever spawned. His payment? Bounty.

Chronicle of a Bounty Hunter

Dave Hooker

A Black Horse Western

ROBERT HALE

© Dave Hooker 2020
First published in Great Britain in 2020

ISBN 978-0-7198-3140-9

The Crowood Press
The Stable Block
Crowood Lane
Ramsbury
Marlborough
Wiltshire SN8 2HR

www.bhwesterns.com

Robert Hale is an imprint
of The Crowood Press

The right of Dave Hooker to be identified as
author of this work has been asserted by him
in accordance with the Copyright, Designs
and Patents Act 1988

Typeset by
Simon and Sons ITES Services Pvt Ltd
Printed and bound in Great Britain by
4Bind Ltd, Stevenage, SG1 2XT

PROLOGUE

In 1854, seven years before the start of the American Civil War, John Harris and his brother Shane are living with their parents somewhere in the Dakotas when a mixed band of renegade Indians, white, and black men destroyed their quarter section homestead. The boys hide in outbuildings for two days until a posse out of Light Foot found them. John is five years old, and Shane is four. Their parents are found dead. All records are lost or destroyed in the fire that burnt the ranch house to the ground. As small children the only traceable relatives the boys have are Aunt Mimi and Uncle Will, in Caspin, Wyoming. The Episcopal Church in Light Foot used Christian influence with the Church in Caspin to locate Mimi and Will, who own a dry goods store in the Wyoming town. The elderly couple agree to take the boys in. The Episcopal Church elders in Light Foot have a member who is influential with the Wells and Fargo stage line. Through this connection the boys are sent far away to Aunt Mimi and Uncle Will.

John and Shane never looked alike and had totally different personalities. Only a year separates them, but because of the terrible experiences they shared the two are bonded by the steel of life. Shane is tubby and gentle by nature as a young boy, but grows tall and lean, yet still gentle, a natural towards farming and nothing like his brother John, who has a dominating personality. Yet together they have grown to be strong friends, happy with Mimi and Will, who were like second parents to them. At sixteen, Shane gets work on a beef ranch twenty-five miles away from Caspin and is only able to come home at weekends. John becomes restless, and at seventeen joins the local militia. The extra money helps out at the store. A lone gunman tries to rob Mimi and Will's dry goods store whilst the boys are away and kills Will. The militia and a posse from Caspin try to capture the gunman but cannot find him. John, with his local knowledge, tells Shane that he aims to track the man down and kill him. Shane is horrified and says he will be hanged if caught. John Harris eventually tracks the killer down, confronts him and when the man bad mouths Will – agreeing that he has killed him in cold blood. John shoots the gunman dead through the heart. There are no witnesses. John returns to the store. Shane is there looking after heartbroken Aunt Mimi and the two young men talk. John, at only 17, says that he shot the gunman dead after he went for his gun. He then confesses to Shane that he was going to kill the man anyway, but the gunfighter drew first. Through this talk with his brother, John Harris comes to his senses and realises that he is now a *gallowsbird*, someone the law could hang as a murderer.

The killer drew his six-gun first, but there is no proof of that. Shane insists that his brother is not a natural killer – but he accepts John has become very good with a Colt revolver.

Soon to be a wanted man if the law links John to the killing, he waits for the dust to settle and then takes off to find a new life, never expecting to see Aunt Mimi or Shane again. He changes his name to Jack Hoffmann. Many adventures build his reputation as a Western gunfighter to be feared. Each encounter grows upon the last: speed legendary; cold cunning beyond measure... Yet does his love for Kate Strong show a tiny weakness?

ONE

Harvey's Hell is a narrow gorge extending into a rocky, high-walled basin. It remains wide enough for three unsuspecting horsemen to travel into it line abreast – at least for a while. The desperate passage of seven riders was deafening as they flew on, drowning out any sound of pursuit. But the posse made up by the good townsfolk of Pardoe Plains wasn't far behind them. The hoodlums hammered on, taking sharp bends with ease, such was their horsemanship, clattering across pebbled streamlets in their headlong run as an early moon commenced its ride across the great Wyoming skies, revealed through a slim gap in the great escarpments all around.

Josh Petersen, the de facto leader of the wild-men gang, had been wondering for weeks now if maybe he wasn't a little too old at twenty-seven to be taking on such mad-dog risks in a career of bank robbery: he could easily change his ways – get a job, or start raising a few cattle with the money he had robbed – settle down to a life where a man might get to live to sixty or seventy, rather than being lucky to see thirty. As they thundered across scrub and scree he came to a sudden decision. Until recently, he had never been the sort of hombre who really planned, or even considered the future beyond the here and now. Josh Petersen used to live for the moment, existing from day to day, because he *had* to risk his all to satisfy a life-urge of deadly risk that had been part of him since childhood. But the thought that it was time to change was now growing in his mind – if he could survive this.

A glimmer of light about a half mile ahead caught his eye and fired his evil mind: it could be nothing at all, the sun was very low beyond the gorge, rock shadows were already stretching high up ahead – when suddenly he remembered this place clearly. He had outrun the law here when he was only seventeen years old. Yes, he realized it, like a bolt from the blue. This was the place all right. The rocky detritus floor was a remnant from pre-history, nothing more, and the apparent trail entered a high-walled basin that had no way out. It went nowhere. It was a trap for anyone fleeing. But there was a narrow crevice that had once saved him, just wide enough to take a rider and horse – if the rider dismounted, quietened the animal and moved like a shadow.

The devious man made an instant decision to leave his six companions to their fate – most had dodgers in sheriffs' offices across Wyoming Territory and beyond, with the instruction '*Wanted, dead or alive*'. They were as good as dead men now, and would be trapped in that high-walled rocky basin, and probably killed there. Not Petersen, he decided, and dropped back at a sharp bend, stopping his lathered horse carefully and dismounting. The sound of pursuit was becoming louder as he calmed the bay and led her charily into the crevice that had once saved his life – and a few seconds later the Pardoe Plains posse thundered by. A few moments' wait to allow for stragglers, and Petersen was up in leather and back out of Harvey's Hell, driven by the evil that now filled his soul.

***

New Hope is a lonesome ghost town that most folks had heard of in stories when they were sat around their evening fires, across Wyoming and Kansas Territories – a desolate place far from any real habitation. A long time past a stage line had once run through there. But not any more. Now all dreams were wasted, blown away on the hot prairie winds. All about lay open scrubland, running unhindered, save for tumbleweed and cacti, to the feet of slate-blue mountains ten miles away, their heights cloud-covered, as winds blew them across the wild, wide prairielands of Wyoming Territory and on to the far distant sea.

Two solitary riders approached from opposite sides of the derelict ghost town, the wind whipping up dust eddies that partially obscured each rider from the other. Josh Petersen was first to arrive in Main Street. He rode slow and careful, not knowing who was there, and primed for some son-of-a-gun to bushwack him. Petersen was tall in the saddle. He wore a full Mexican-style moustache, the hard planes of his face half hidden in shade under a black Stetson, from under which two diamond-sharp blue eyes flickered cautiously around.

The two men had arranged this meeting. They were half-brothers. Two of four boys who had seen many years' hard work, both day and night, as their family struggled for survival on their quarter-section farm. Sleep and food became a luxury after Josh Petersen's father had been hung for cattle rustling in Wheatland in June 1873 – a seeming hot-spot for such final punishment. Then, the only man in the family, a newcomer, Herbert Stephens, ran off with another man to seek his fortune.

This cruel start indelibly marked Stoler and Petersen, and these two half-brothers became born survivors. Their hard baptism in life had forced many compromises: one credo that had soon disappeared from their moral depository was the decency of Western neighbourliness – unwritten laws out there on the frontier lands – the 'howdy stranger, set a spell, eat and drink your fill' attitude of the homesteaders, helping to build the creed that made an enduring imprint on the American legend. For the brothers, giving of themselves for any reason was only temporary, while taking had become the only reality. Life had done its best to make the two brothers evil, and they had succumbed with everything they had.

Petersen tied his appaloosa horse to the worn hitching rail outside the once raucous Western Dreams saloon – the batwings were still there, squeaking to and fro on the wind that came whistling down Main Street. The range rider shouldered his way through with a gunny sack over his shoulder. The long room was laid out in two parts, one for gambling, one for drinking and whoring – but the steps to rooms upstairs allocated for the latter had all but gone. Petersen sat down at the one table left standing and waited for his older half-brother to arrive. The two men, now full grown, hadn't got on in the past, but money – gold, to be precise – together with a not insignificant amount of greed, had brought them back to meet up in this sad and dead place.

Mordecai Stoler soon shouldered through the batwing doors and smiled cunningly. He was dressed in dusty range gear like his brother and said with a tightly controlled smile out of a large, bearded face: 'You look as handsome as ever, Joshua.'

'As ever…' Josh gritted his teeth obviously, opened the gunny sack and took out a bag of gold dust.

His half-brother's eyes nearly popped out of the ugly head. He wiped a large nose with a dirty kerchief and stared at the gold.

'Did you bring measuring scales, like I said?'

Mordecai dropped his head apologetically. 'I knew you were kin and could be trusted, Joshua…' His eyes glinted with pleasure at his own slick words.

Petersen pulled out a small prospector's scales and set them up. 'There. Exactly as I promised you. Five ounces of pure gold dust. Now we're even. But I want something from you in return, brother!'

Mordecai grabbed the gold greedily and put it in a burlap bag hanging over his shoulder. The light of triumph faded from his devious eyes, and he settled back on the rickety chair. 'I've found out a lot – just as you asked. But I've got a question for you first! What happened with your gang? Heard they all got killed, everyone but you?' He smirked as if he was enjoying the pain of an enemy, not kin folk.

'Yeah. They're all dead except me, Mordecai.' Joshua took out a leather water bottle from the gunny sack at his side, and Mordecai did the same from the bag on his shoulder. When Petersen had drunk his fill, he continued: 'Three were killed in the fight with the posse, holed up as they were in a rock basin at the end of that danged hell-hole gulch. There was no way out for them. Floyd Fisher, Tom Weeks an' Big Bill Smythe were captured an' hung back in Pardoe Plains a few days later. The town council had already set up a hanging machine – you knows the type, hangs up to six fellas at a time. Well, dang me, if they didn't hang Floyd, Tom and Bill as soon as they got back, along with some others held in the sheriff's cells. Immediate, like.' He glared. 'Something to do with the trouble they all had setting up that darn machine in the first place. Anyway, they did at least give them a fair trial afterwards…'

Mordecai nodded, grinning, 'I suppose we ought to be grateful for that brother, fair trial and all. Makes you proud to be part of this great Frontier Territory…' He built a quirly skilfully with nimble fingers, then pushed the pouch of strong Bull Durham tobacco across to his brother. 'My turn to tell, eh?' He banged his dusty hat on his leg, threw it on the table and lifted his sun-burned head, which had seen much ducking and diving across an ill-gotten life, the long, brown-flaked nose helping to give him a strange appearance of importance in his otherwise devious demeanour. His dirty brown eyes held Josh Petersen's hard blue ones.

'You want to start up anew, I guess? No more bank robberies, eh, so I've heard? Besides, your gang's dead and in hell anyway. Now you want to become a gunfighter, a new career, a gun for hire, so brother Daniel tells me. That right?'

'Bin practisin' a mite out on the prairie in a small gulch tucked away off the trail. Always was pretty handy with a six-shooter. Got better with practice. But I ain't no gunslick, Mordecai.' He winked. 'An' I ain't no fool either. There's got to be faster men than me out there, no matter how much I practises and how good I gets. Figure I done well out of pulling bank raids, got quite a bit stashed, but what with me being the only one left now, I gotta change, Mordecai. Gunsel living is OK, but not for too long, in case I meets up with a real hot-shot.'

'Like Jack Hoffmann?'

'Yeah. Like that son-of-a-bitch. You got a plan then?'

'Oh, I gotta plan, Joshua. I got a real good one… but I wants something for it!' Mordecai leaned forwards on the table, and its rotten state creaked back. 'This here gold of yours has bought you something special, brother.' He lifted the bag of gold dust out of the shoulder bag with his left hand, and pulled out a bottle filled with rye whiskey with the other; then he took out two whiskey glasses, and slid a glass and the bottle across to Joshua.

'Take yersel' a snort.' The two men began drinking. Suddenly it was like old times, before they had fallen out.

TWO

'Jack Hoffmann is as good as he ever was.' Mordecai Stoler smiled darkly at his brother. 'Killed more men than any gunsel I've ever known. Every killing is legal. He always lets them draw first, but he's always quicker to killing position. He'll kill you as easy as winking, Joshua. An' if you did get a shot in somehow and missed, he'd finish ya with ol' Betsy, that short-ened scattergun on his other hip.' Stoler's tough, range-hardened arms pushed the overweight body back into the protesting chair.

'But not if you have a real good plan, which I'm going to give you, where you never have to stand before Jack Hoffmann or any other gunfighter, yet still get to get a powerful gunfighter's reputation – which, as you will see, will help us both in the best robbery this Territory has ever seen – if you are care-ful and do just as I say. But I wants my cut for this, as we will come to. Make your money with your gun as you wants – gold is the best currency I know – take it and the gold we're going to rob, then move out to Californy before you're caught by the law or some-one quicker than you. I want to come with you to

Californy, sort of brotherly love to look after you – get my drift?' The bearded face smiled slickly.

'But first you need a rep as a gunfighter for my plan ta work. Like I say, you won't have to confront no one. And my plan's the very one to boost your name across this here Goodland County as a real good gunfighter.'

The two badmen looked at each other, both unsure of the other, but with greedy optimism fired. Mordecai Stoler pulled on his quirly, smoke surrounding his bearded, ugly head. You know Hardin's Bluff well?'

'No. No reason to go there. Jack Hoffmann hangs out at some saloon, I believe. Why look for trouble in the back yard of that dangerous varmint?'

'Well, Joshua, I can tell you that Hoffmann will be away from the Midnight Star on some long bounty trip soon. I was just passing through Hardin's Bluff a month or so ago and wanted some beer an' vittles, so I stops in that there Star saloon. Hoffmann was there, but I paid him no account, and he paid me none. Then all of a sudden there's gunfire right outside, an' some fella's a-calling out a dude sitting no farther from me than I could spit. "Come out of there Mal Quincy, you coward," the voice says. "Show me how quick on the draw you really are!"'

Mordecai Stoler tells his half brother of these events in ice-cool detail from direct experience, because he was in the Midnight Star on that eventful day, together with what he could pick up in the chatter of townsfolk only too pleased to talk about it. This was the story:

Jack Hoffmann got up and sauntered grimly across the bar room, everyone, including Mordecai Stoler, watching transfixed. Hoffmann was a big man, dressed, when at ease, in a worn leather vest and check shirt, blue jeans and dusty boots – yet he always wore the deadly gun-rig he was known for, a polished .45 Colt tied down on his right hip and the shortened scattergun on the left. Jack Hoffmann shouldered his way through the batwings and looked across the beaten-down dirt road to the would-be gunslinger.

'Howdy. Want no gun fighting here in Hardin's Bluff,' said Hoffmann in a deep voice like black molasses. As usual he looked hard as hell, with no emotion on him. 'Sheriff's outa town now. He'll be back in a spell.'

'I guessed you'd be out here first to protect that little varmint. I'm a law-abiding citizen. You knows the law as well as me, Mr Hoffmann. I ain't got no quarrel with you. Just want Western justice for my kin. Mal Quincy gunned down my kid brother for no good reason at all. Get him out here to stand before me, man to man like, an' well see whose fastest on the draw.'

'Yup. Guess you're right about the law, but only in part. The law also says if you draws first and kills someone, that's murder, an' you'll hang as sure as the sun be a-setting in this big Wyoming sky.'

The cowboy fell to silence. He was dressed in dusty range gear with a black Stetson set well on his head; he was smoking a small black cheroot between his teeth, but he spat it out.

'OK, Mr Hoffmann, I knows the law too. Get him out here an' we'll finish this for good.'

Behind Hoffmann the sound of the batwings sliding past careful shoulders caused the big man to turn quickly.

'I killed your brother in a fair fight.' Mal Quincy stood with seemingly no sign of fear about him. Of medium height and build, the gunfighter was dressed for the image: black pants, black shirt, polished boots and a brown leather vest. The low-crowned Stetson was as immaculate as was he. He carried a pearl-handled 45-calibre British Tranter tied down on his left hip, cross-draw style. 'Pat drew on me first, an' I had to defend myself.'

Jack Hoffmann stood back.

Mal Quincy smiled. 'Lookee-here. I can see you're a fair guy. And I don't want to kill you for nothing. So I'm gonna draw first, just to wing you, friend.' Quincy grinned. 'Just to make my point that you're too slow for me. You're just a backwater guy who's got carried away a mite. Mr Hoffmann here will know I done it for the good of us both. Yoose can buy me a drink after.'

What happened next became a legend across the West.

Jacob Moses drew his Colt in a split second of time as Mal Quincy lifted his six-gun free of the tooled holster; squatting low, Moses fanned the hammer to flame just once with the edge of his hand. The proud gunfighter had hardly cleared leather when a slug entered his chest and drove him back over on to his stomach, blood and gore across the dirt road.

A moment's silence reigned. Then drinkers, card players, shop keepers came out of the Midnight Star saloon and shops to stare at the new gunfighter and with astonished talk, some bravely slapping Moses on the back.

'Hold it!' The dominating figure of Jack Hoffmann cut a swathe through the crowd and he put a large, strong hand on Moses' shoulder. 'Holster that gun, now.' The young man did as he was bid, the forty-five still smoking. With that, Jack Hoffman led the cowboy in through the batwings, through the bar room and down into Kate Strong's parlour at the back, acknowledging her as he went.

'Set yourself down, mister. I want to talk to you.' Dark eyes held Jacob Moses like a vice. Yet he was man enough not to be cowed and sat down on a beautifully crafted chair, clearly from out East. The room was immaculate, gold and blue drapes at the windows, carpets on the floor, in direct contrast to everything the tough range world held beyond its door.

Hoffmann stared coldly at the young cowboy. 'Outside them batwings, folks will be talking like there's no tomorrow, son.' The big man got up nimbly and took out two glasses from Kate's drinks cabinet, set them down and filled the glasses from a crystal decanter. 'Suddenly, in a twinkling, you've become Jacob Moses who out-gunned Mal Quincy, a serious gunfighter who I know for sure the Sheriff of this here town has a dodger on. That dead guy out there in the dust is your passport to fame, glory, an' an early death in a year or two. I knows what I'm a-talking about. Killing is my business, Mr Moses.' Silence reigned for some long seconds. 'I do it because I do it; for bounty dollars to live, if the guy the law wants won't come in peaceable. And to even the balance sometimes between the good folks and the bad. One day I'll have to stop when I slows, or end up like Mal Quincy out there in the dirt. I can tell you're quick on the draw, as you've just proven to us all. But someone will soon find you and take your rep from you, Mr Moses – which means you'll

21

be dead as Mal Quincy is now out there.' Jack Hoffmann lifted his glass. 'Here's to you, friend.'

Jacob Moses got to his feet and they both snorted the red-eye together.

'I wants you to leave this here town and let things settle. Where do you call home?'

'Tomlinson.'

'Well, get yourself back there, forget this day, and I'll do my best to play the whole thing down. Can't promise much. The word is out that there's a new gunfighter out there some-where on the prairie or in Western towns, and it'll be com-mon knowledge by tomorrow. But you must let it be known that you don't keep a gun on your hip any more. Give what-ever reason you want. That's what I want you to do.' Both men stared hard. 'What do you say, Mr Moses?'

Jacob Moses looked hard into those dark eyes again – there was death there, and something else he could not quite dis-cern. 'You make a lot o' sense Mr Hoffmann. A lot. When Quincy killed my brother, I was all tied up in anger after-wards. Pat was more than just a kid brother. I couldn't see how I was to continue with our small spread alone. Sure I've got some hired hands. But they're drifters. On my own... don't know how I'll survive, you know.'

Hoffmann refilled their glasses. 'Life makes some folks bad 'cos they sees it as the only way forward. I can under-stand that. But the good struggles on to find a way through. I think you're one o' them who struggles on...'

Jacob Moses said nothing and took a snort of his whiskey.

'Let's leave it there, friend. Where's your horse? Out at the hitching rail?'

Jacob nodded.

'I suggest you gets up into leather tomorrow morn and heads back to – where did you say?'

'Tomlinson.'

'Yeah. Tomlinson, an' forget this ever happened. You can stay here in the Star overnight, courtesy o' Kate Strong – I'll have a word.'

It seemed from common knowledge that Jack Hoffmann had a streak in him that no one could quite see or understand. This dealer of death had a small measure of compassion, or so it seemed – at least bound up in his own rules for life. Very occasionally, if he liked a man who was starting out on a path to naïve glory, he would try to dissuade him and give some guidance. If he got nowhere, Hoffmann would find a way of killing the man who had proved he was bad or very stupid with ruthless efficiency. 'You are too dangerous to live' was the justification of his actions.

THREE

'A happy ending.' Josh lit up his quirly. 'Jack Hoffmann has a way in him that might be good, or it might be bad. Either way he'll kill a fella and not lose any sleep over it. So where do I come in to this, Mordecai?'

'This is where we git really clever, brother. An' rather devious, I'm a-proud ta say.' Mordecai took a snort of red-eye. 'You see, I knows that Kate Strong's a real clever lady. Yessir. Not only is she clever and tough, running the Star likes she does, an' having Jack Hoffmann as her lover, so's no hard case muscles in on her property – she also has, by pure luck, one of her kin working as an operator at one o' them new-fangled telegraph offices over Harpersville way. Years ago, she loaned fifty dollars to a stage-coach driver. He wuz married with five kids – all gals, poor guy, and one was a-dying from dehydration an' something poisonous she ate whilst out picking plants for the family ta eat. The girl's ma was desperate for doctoring. He never forgot Kate's generosity that probably saved the gal's life. So if Jack Hoffmann's name comes down the telegraph line, Paddy, the telegraph operator, sends it through to Kate at the Midnight Star.'

The two fell to silence.

'Don't underestimate her. Ever. She uses her money to get things done. Money talks. So when Jack pulls in some loot, whether it be legit, from bounty payment, or from folks who's paid him for badmen stopped, Jack pays her bills an' more, as a thank you for keeping the wheels of her businesses turning and him ahead of events.'

'How do you know all this, Mord? I've known you all my life. Never knew yer was so darned clever.'

The big, slippery face grinned. 'Oh, I ain't clever, not book learning, anyways. But I knows lots o' folks' secrets, like, and I'm devious, you might say, and proud of it, like I can get in any house, big or small, open most safes easy as winking. And no one ever knows I was there! All this stuff good folks don't speak about, I gets to know, though – an' sometimes I can pick up on something big. That's how's I knows about Hoffmann, his tart, an' the goings on around the Midnight Star. I knows what I knows…

'And I tells ya, it'll be a long, long time afore he returns to the Star. If he does! Yer see, Hoffmann's accepted a bounty contract to stop the Gene Pinder gang from stealin' a shipment of gold in Sharack County, that's being taken to Lusk rail-head on a strengthened, heavy wagon. Needs six head o' horses, so I'm told, just to pull that there wagon along, 'cos it's got so much gold on it. He only gets paid when the job's done. An' I knows they're on the outlook for talent – both the good guys working for the federal government, and the bad guys liken us, who wants to take it from them!' Stoler roared with laughter.

Josh Petersen pushed back his black Stetson. 'I knows Pinder. Fact is, we and Tom Wolff together done a heist down Wichita way, years ago.'

Stoler relit his quirly as the batwings banged ominously in the wind, and he slid the whiskey bottle over to his half-brother, who filled his glass again and stroked thumb and forefinger thoughtfully over the black, drooping moustache. 'Say, what yer got in mind for me to win this here gunfighter rep?'

'Patience, bro'. For Hoffmann to do his stuff to stop the gold heist, he must first meet up with some others, useful boys, an' set things up. Don't know how or where. We got some time yet afore that strengthened wagon is full of gold for us.' Mordecai leaned forwards conspiratorially on to the creaking table: 'This is where the clever part begins an' why I wants to go with you to Californy and get my cut of this here plan. I've put a lot of work in.'

'How would I get the fellow's rep without a-killing him?' Joshua Petersen looked hard at his kin. 'That'll make me a target for a hanging judge.'

'Like Judge Parker?'

'Yeah. He'll do.'

'Not a chance, brother. I'll tells you why.'

The two paused and stared at each other.

'Jacob Moses has done what Jack Hoffmann advised. He's back on his small spread near Tomlinson. No guns. An' apart from a hired hand or two, he's all alone.'

Mordecai emptied the last of his red-eye into his whiskey glass and belched. 'Beggin' yer pardon an' all,' he offered. That slimy smile crossed his face, then vanished in a moment. 'This here telegraph operator who is kin with Kate Strong, is called Paddy Flynn. He and I did a spell in Kirkwood prison together. Nasty place, so it is, as Paddy would say. If the telegraph folks ever found out about Paddy's past, he'd be out on his ass, what with telegraph secrecy being so important and all. Paddy knows I've got something' big on him, should I want to talk. Which I don't. We meet up for a beer now and then when I pass through Michaeltown, an' he gives out bits an' pieces that might interest me to keep me sweet and my mouth shut, as you might say. That's how I found out about this here heist with Gene Pinder down Sharack way.'

'Well, dang me. You never told me about that, either.' Josh Petersen got up and walked around the creaking floor of the derelict saloon, shaken by what he had missed with someone as close to him as Mordecai, his own half-brother. He suddenly turned and bore down on Mordecai.

Mordecai grinned. 'Yoose fancy an easy ride over ta Tomlinson?'

'What you got in mind?'

'Cos that's where you're going to pick up a gun-fighter's reputation as easy as snorting a shot o' red-eye. All you've got to do is find Jacob Moses when he's alone on his spread...' Mordecai took out a bundle of stolen dollar bills tied up with hessian string from his burlap bag and dropped the bundle on the table.

'That county hick will never have seen so much money in all his life. Wave my bundle o' bills at him, and keep sitting on your horse. Tell him quite openly that you want his reputation as a gunfighter and are willing to pay handsomely for it. Let him know your name is Joshua Petersen.

'All he wants in the world is to take Hoffmann's advice an' rid himself of the gunfighter reputation. That I now know for sure. He sounds like a clever fella an' doesn't want to die. You tell Jacob Moses that if he wants this money, to tell everyone the following story.

'Say that a man turned up out of nowhere, said his name was Joshua Petersen, he remained sitting on his horse with a six-gun on his hip. The man demanded that Jacob put on his gun-rig and challenged him to a fast draw. If he didn't the gunman would shoot him dead on the spot. People will understand that there was no choice. Western gun law. The stranger wins the draw – make that quite clear – but the bullet only grazed the side of your head, Jacob. This man then rode off like the wind, obviously thinking that Jacob Moses, the man laying on the ground with the great rep as a gunfighter, wuz dead,.' Mordecai smiled that evil smile.

'Tell him that to earn the bundle of dollars you've given him for his reputation, he must never reveal the truth, and that he must become the rancher who never uses a gun, as he wants to be.'

Josh took his off his Stetson and pushed it over his back, Mexican style, and re-lit his quirly with a red match struck on the heel of his boot. Mordecai finished up with saying:

'Don't yer worry none, Joshua. The way that guy moved an' spoke out front of the Midnight Star, he created a rep that's a real powerful crowd puller, an' it's already travelled far an' wide – Jacob Moses, the country boy who outgunned the famous Mal Quincy! It's worth every dollar in that bundle I'm a-givin' yer.'

The batwing doors clattered. It was the only sound in that crumbling bar room.

'Got two questions for yer, Mord. The first is, what's ta stop me ridin' off with that there bundle o' money an' never see ya again? Second is, why should ya go ta so much trouble ta get me a rep as a gunman? Brotherly love?'

Mordecai replied easily. He had thought out his plan very well. 'Brotherly love?' He smiled a supercilious smile. 'Of course, kid brother. With a gunfighter's reputation like you will have gotten yourself, Gene Pinder will be only too pleased to have you in his gang. You will have a scary reputation and can demand a big number o' them gold bars in the heist. And who's going to argue with you? Don't think Jacob Moses will give you any trouble with the real

29

truth. He just wants shot of the whole business. He's got more dollar bills than he ever dreamed of having, everyone's expecting him to stay clear o' guns anyways. He don't want no more gunfighters looking for him, either. Your face won't be on any sheriff's dodgers. And Pinder ain't gonna argue about your rep none – he just wants the gold. And the dollars? Got a lot more of them from the stagecoach hold-up and I'm willing to gamble some of it for our future in Californy.

'I've set up a gold-for-dollars exchange with a few different guys who have the ability to melt down them there gold bars, an' don't ask too many questions, either. Believe me, Joshua, they are real experienced in the business. Then you and me will be free to go to Californy or wherever yuh like with our considerable loot, and be rich. Very rich! No one suspecting a thing!'

The two brothers looked at each other, a faint smile appearing on each disreputable face.

'Where's this small spread that Jacob Moses runs?'

Mordecai knew at that moment he had won the first round. 'A few miles south-west of Tomlinson. You can't miss it, Joshua.'

'And where will I find the Gene Pinder gang?'

Mordecai had everything worked out to the last detail and smiled. 'Have you heard of the mine off the road from Fort Carmin to Lusk? They say Morgan Reeves robbed a stagecoach stopping there with dollars on board for the miners' pay. There was a riot, and afterwards it fell on hard times.'

'You think you can find it?'

Joshua Petersen nodded. 'I can find any place that suits.'

'Well, that's where Pinder is based, in the buildings of that old mine.'

'When are you leaving, bro?'

The tyro gunfighter grinned. 'Go back to my shack first, pick up travelling gear, and then off. I'll meet you at Primer Lodge afterwards in a months time. It's on the Lusk road. We'll begin our plans for the gold bars. Pinder know you and me. We'll work it out between us. That all right with you Mordecai?'

They both laughed heartily.

***

At that moment, outside the Midnight Star in Hardin's Bluff, a tall, slim man rode up. A little underweight from hard work rather than shortage of food, he got down from his sorrel mare, tied her carefully to the hitching rail, and entered through the batwing doors. A few people were inside, some drinking, some eating good provision that was still made, or at least over-seen, by Kate Strong, the saloon's owner. She stood behind the bar with Thomas, the barkeep, and was polishing glasses with him.

'Is this the right place for Jack Hoffmann, and if so, can I speak with him, please?' he said cautiously.

Kate looked up into a kindly young face that had been worn down a little by life. His sandy hair was thinning, grey, thoughtful eyes were tired but shone resolutely out of a weather-beaten face that was full of character, and although the stranger had a well-defined square jaw and very firmly delineated mouth to support the character type, she registered immediately that there was concern, almost fear there.

'Who shall I say is calling?' For some reason that she could not account for, the man's face and his distinctive demeanour felt strangely familiar.

Shane Harris found himself trapped for the moment by a pair of strong green eyes, red hair, and the woman's beautiful but very tough face that had clearly seen a lot of life. 'Shane Harris,' he replied a little self-consciously.

She gave him a strange look of caution. 'And the reason?'

'Personal.'

Jack Hoffmann was sitting at a roll-top desk writing with a quill pen and an open ink pot beside his many papers; the new fountain pens, still questioned by some as worthwhile, had not yet reached the frontier town. He turned from his easy reverie to see the door wide open and Kate with the stranger beside her.

'Yes?'

More than five years had passed since the brothers had last seen each other. Shane was a cattleman now. A successful rancher who took an establishment view on life. And in spite of the dusty ride, it showed. The door closed. 'Don't you know me, John?'

Jack Hoffmann had developed a façade of tough neutrality. He gave nothing away on his face – ever. Then slowly the years faded, and he found himself looking into the mature face of his only brother. But the steely neutrality stood the test, the gunfighter didn't buckle, gave nothing away.

'Had a hell of a job finding you. I knew you were going to change your name, so I couldn't give anything away in my asking. So don't worry on that none. Been nearly two week's riding, going over past places until I had a hunch that Hardin's Bluff might be the place.'

Hoffmann smiled suddenly, got to his feet and opened Kate's drinks cabinet, poured two whiskeys and bid Shane to sit on the other side of a beautiful drop-leaf table near a tall window. 'You must have a mighty good reason to find me, Shane. Come straight to the point: what is this visit all about?'

Shane Harris wasn't fazed by his brother's directness. This was typical of him. No 'hello brother, good to see you after all this time, how is Aunt Mimi these days?' Nothing. Shane sat still, a little affronted nonetheless. He gathered himself and took the only approach he knew his brother would accept. 'We need a tough gunfighter to help the citizenry win our town back from thugs and gunmen who have taken it over.'

'Caspin? Can't the law help?'

'It's not Caspin, Jack. Aunt Mimi died years ago. I have a friend in the Wells and Fargo office. He reckoned we have kin in a frontier town way out west, called Longhorn. I've got work out there on a ranch and live there now.'

'Kin?'

'Yes, sir. Distant cousins of ours and the like.'

Hoffmann's dark eyes swung back at his brother. 'Don't need no kin.' The big man got to his feet, walked over to the door, opened it and asked for the barkeep or swamper to bring them in a big pot of hot coffee and cups. He returned to his seat. 'Knows you don't like hard liquor, brother. I can take either.'

Shane nodded. 'Thanks, Jack. I'll call you that from now on. Have no worries about that.'

Soon the steaming coffee pot was before them, dainty cups and saucers and a sugar bowl.

'When we were boys I could see you took to ciphering and spelling, like a coot to the pond. So I'm gonna tell you what's happened to me, Jack, and the other ranchers and business around Longhorn town, with some figure work in it. Know you'll understand. I have a mortgage from the bank out there on a little house. Normal rates when I signed my papers a year ago. All was well, hard work for myself and Judy, we done well enough. Oh yeah, I got a wife now. Then the McCormack gang showed up, subtle like at first.' His grey eyes burned.

'Five of them arrived here from Kansas, packing a lot of money and guns. Within a week, they took control of the bank and saloon. Most of the land and businesses were already in debt to the bank, as it held their deeds. Ezra McCormack took over – said he was kin to the manager. No proof on it, though. Silas Smith the real bank manager vanished. No one saw hide nor hair of him go. Just disappeared. There one moment, vanished the next. McCormack increased the interest rate until a few people went broke. This will allow him to resell those properties and make a tidy profit – if we don't stop him in time, and real quick.

'There's no law yet in Longhorn, so we couldn't do anything but watch. The circuit judge would arrive every now and then. Said law would arrive soon, but it never did. Then suddenly we got a sheriff who was one of the gang. Took over Widow Peggity's rooming house as a front with lots o' rooms to store things – guns, ammo and the like – and she was paid off through the newly run bank. Widow Peggity left on a stagecoach heading down Laramie ways, and it was all paid for by the bank.'

Jack Hoffmann poured two strong black coffees and nodded at Shane. 'Go on, bro.'

'That's when all the ranchers and other businesses got notice that our mortgage repayments were going to be increased by twenty-five per cent. Also a twenty-five per cent tax was to be levied on every business in town. The bank upped mortgages and loans that had been granted at ten per cent to twenty-five per cent the following month. The bank holds all our deeds, so what could we do? Except go into town and see the new bank manager, Ezra McCormack! There was a load of us all a-waitng to see him, and that's when the dime dropped. The new sheriff called Henderson, he turns up with some toughs he reckons he's deputised, and threatens to throw us all in jail for breaking the peace when new cells are completed in a few days' time.' Shane drained his coffee cup and looked at the coffee pot.

Jack refilled both cups.

'Already the foreclosures on local properties are being arranged. So we all had a meeting at Micky Dobson's ranch house, because it's the biggest, and he soon took the lead in this business. We formed a trial committee. Like you, Jack, he has a real good business head on his shoulders – least ways, he's used it for business, not anything else!'

Shane shot a look at Jack over the rim of his coffee cup to see dark eyes burning at him, but no reaction. 'Anyways, Micky is a good and clever man who tried to send word out to Harpersville, who now possess a law officer, that we're in a real mess. The rider was brought back across his horse. One of the McCormack gang brought him back. We can't get word out to the authorities. Seems we have to take this gang into custody ourselves as a citizens' arrest. Lock them up in this newly being built jail house and send for the county sheriff and advise the circuit judge as to what has happened.'

Jack Hoffman snorted his whiskey. 'Sounds all right to me…'

Shane's grey eyes blinked for a moment. His firm jaw tightened more. 'You've missed something, brother,' he hissed. 'Not one man jack of us is a gunman. Those toughs are part of the McCormack gang. There's a number of them who are not gunslingers, it's true. But a lot are! Like I said, some have taken properties, the Buffalo Saloon, the bank, and a new sheriff has set himself up, also the town's mayor position. The crittas are everywhere now in town. Seems they've taken over. The deputies are led by the Coyote Kid. You heard of him?'

Hoffmann's harsh face didn't change a muscle. He just nodded. Then said, 'The man's mighty quick.'

'So now you can see why I'm here.'

'Business.'

'Yeah. Business.' Shane had hoped for a touch of kin folks' feeling from his only brother, but got none.

'I can't offer you the sort of money you are used to – in fact I'm empowered by our committee to offer you no more than sixty dollars, what with foreclosures an' all.'

Shane's gunfighter brother sat statue still for a long while, then said, 'Charity. You want charity, then?'

'We're kin. Thought you might want to help a town out of a lingering death.' Shane filled his cup from the pot. 'Like I explained afore, the bank will repossess the properties that have a default against them, because they hold the deeds, and then sell them on. We're doing our best as a town to stop these places being sold – hand them back to their true owners if this McCormack gang can be stopped. When they've grabbed enough loot the whole gang will move on. Kill a town, steal their money and ride away, afore the law can do anything to stop them. Apparently they've been doing this all over. Before the law can reach a newly sprouted community, they clean it dry! The new homesteaders who've paid for the foreclosed properties in good faith will be duped. Thank God we've not got any sales yet.'

Jack Hoffmann nodded slowly. 'OK. I'll see what I can do. Go back and see this Micky Dobson, your committee head.' His voice was deep and mellow. 'Say I'll want to stay a while at his spread. Get him to convene a committee meeting, and we'll all talk some. Can't say anything will come of it, though.'

'How much money do you want for this work?'

'Sixty dollars up front. That's what you're offering, ain't it?'

'Yep. But I ain't got that sort of money with me, Jack.'

The big man gave a very rare smile. 'Seeing as you're kin, I'll trust you, Shane. I'm willing to ride to Longhorn outskirts and arrive at your Micky Dobson's ranch in two weeks. You be there with sixty dollars up front, and we'll make a start.' Hoffmann knew that he had also given his word to deal with the gold heist in Sharack County whilst it was being taken to Lusk rail-head on a strengthened, heavy wagon. But there was enough time – just – for this kin folks' job as well, as it was on the way, if he could help them with his experience.

Shane smiled openly. 'Thanks, brother. I'll go one better. Outside of town there's a sign that says simply, Longhorn. It's got a few bullet holes in it. I'll meet you there at two o'clock sharp on Trinity Sunday in two weeks. After church it's snooze time for those lucky enough to get it. Sunday is still the Sabbath – even out here – so that's the best time for the committee to meet at the Double D spread when things is quiet. I'll take you along to meet Micky and our committee, they'll be very pleased to meet you.'

FOUR

Jack Hoffman strode down Main Street in Hardin's Bluff the day before Trinity Sunday. His long strides were easy, his silver spurs jingling with the steps. It was early in the day. He was dressed in his range gear: a fringed buckskin jacket, black pants, with close-fitting leather chaps flapping gently against his legs as he walked. The sun was up in another clear blue sky, and he squinted out from under the brim of a low-crowned black Stetson at townsfolk who pointed him out to friends and whispered words to awe-filled children. He was known in the frontier town as 'the bounty hunter', but there was more to him than that. Hoffmann touched the brim of his hat to acknowledge respectful tidings of the day as folks passed by carefully. He strode on past the blacksmith, the offices of the town newspaper, a large lumber-penned corral and then turned into the livery stables.

'Good morning to you, Mr Hoffmann. Mighty fine day again.' The ostler, a short, stocky man with a thin, close-cropped beard, was well known to the gunfighter, having moved from Indian Wells to flourishing Hardin's Bluff, where business was booming.

As usual he showed his pleasure at giving good service, smiled and indicated to the stall where Jess was waiting.

The livery stables smelled of good clean straw, and the horse snickered a welcome. She had been curried, and looked the better for it. He tacked her up with a rawhide bridle and his McClellan saddle that he took from a beam to the side and from an oak platform built for tack in the corner of the stall, and then strapped the saddle holster in place.

'Like I done said before, Mr Hoffmann, that's a mighty fine saddle you got. A McClellan, ain't it?'

The tall man nodded. 'Bought it from an army store down Blueberg way.'

The ostler smiled in contentment as he leaned against the door. 'When I was in the cavalry I rode hundreds of miles on one just like that. Property of the army. Could have bought it when I finished my time.' He gave a wistful look. 'Wish I had one now.'

Hoffmann tightened the cinches. He paid the ostler and led Jess from the stall. The horse came out of the livery with her coat gleaming, ears pricked and alert. Taking one look back down Main Street to the Midnight Star, the gunfighter swung up into leather, and headed out of Hardin's Bluff on what could prove to be a desperate mission involving his own kin, something he had left behind as a bad memory years before. Jack Hoffmann had sworn to himself he would never return to them. The only things he needed was his lover Kate Strong, his gun-rig, and Jess his horse. Safer that way. No kin. No ties.

He followed a dusty trail for over a day to where the land started to rise in a steady climb. Horse and rider stopped at a ridge marking the beginnings of vast, untouched lands full of forests, chaparral heathlands, rivers and wide-open skies, all completely virginal and free. Wild vines and giant ferns grew up there among the higher reaches. Hoffmann turned Jess and stopped; sitting completely still, he looked back, admiring the scene before him. To his left was a sea of faint waving grasses that fanned out to become part of the great Wyoming plain, which, seen from here, dissipated into ruptures, skylines and castles of white cloud. Hidden in the distant haze was Indian Wells, the small frontier town where he had first settled alone, and where they had wanted to make him sheriff after he had killed Joshua Soames and destroyed his gang of robbers. But closeness and kin folks were not the gunfighter's style, so he had moved on once more.

He patted Jess. 'Come on, girl,' he said, and quietly turned the horse back up the trail. There was an eternal peace there, not from the gentle wind that had picked up some and was now soughing through the trees in easy pleasure, but from the spirit of the place. The range-hardened man could almost smell life's essence, the emptiness and freedom. But there was so much more, and enjoyment filled him like nothing else could.

They rode on at a constant, solid pace for three hours, among thickets of American oak, stands of aspen, changing scenes of elm, pine and cedarwood.

The vistas of powerful beauty were enhanced by the wildflowers of the West: Jacob's ladder, pineland blueberry, black-eyed Susan, rose mallow, among many. Hoffmann's knowledge was not through book learning, but what he had heard tell from tough range men and women who struggled to survive on quarter-section farms, or who had arrived by wagon trains, or were sipping red eye in the Midnight Star. He thought of their words now, where toughness of body and spirit had been exchanged for survival, it seemed. But within these frontier people still ran a true love of the natural world, though it had been mixed with a gut-hardened wisdom of the wild, which sometimes seemed to want them dead when winter storms blew.

The range rider broke for camp soon after noon, when the sun was overhead and at its hottest. Man and horse had followed a natural winding path path through thorn bushes, which led to a large, wildflower meadow. He had used this spot before in the wild lands, and walked the horse through green pasture, dotted with beeves and bighorn sheep that had escaped their herded existence under man's control. As Jess walked, knocking the heads off taller plants, a multitude of butterflies and moths lifted into the air, becoming a fluttering cloud of colour at her flanks. Skylarks also rose and flittered away in zig-zag flight, singing out at the easy approach of the mare.

Hoffmann led Jess down to a small stream and let her drink her fill, then tethered her under a broad oak full of early summer foliage. Then he took a small nosebag containing oats from one of his gunny sacks, hooked it gently on to the horse's head and let her eat. He had a fire ablaze in minutes with dry pieces of mountain grasses and cedarwood; a pot of fresh coffee was soon bubbling on the campfire, and a plate of beef jerky and hot beans tasted good. Jess snickered gently, as if aware of the sun's progress, and the big man climbed to his feet, tossed the remains of the coffee on the fire, stamped it out and packed his few things away. Soon he was up in leather once more, reined the horse back on to the trail and headed up a flinty path.

They topped the hill a few minutes later. From here a wonderful view lay all about. Across that wild, untamed hillside, juniper and piñon, bobbing flowers and wild arrays of mountain laurel and mountain azalea took the hardened range man's breath away. The gunfighter sat still for a long moment, then rode downwards on the trail easily and carefully, man and horse as one. They continued through forested land and open prairie. All around them was a sea of waving grasses, the wind soughing quietly through them, with buttercups and cornflowers peeking out here and there. The spoor of bear, mountain sheep and deer could be seen beneath the trees as they made their way onwards, and after the coolness of the highlands the air was warmer now, yet still fresh and clean. Jack Hoffmann was relaxed on his McClellan saddle and at ease with the world; that virginal part of Wyoming Territory held no fear for him: humanity was too far away for that.

He was approaching Longhorn, and as it came nearer, the bounty hunter felt his honed sense of self-preservation chipping away at his joy. It was nothing the rational mind could account for. He had had this experience before, and simply went along with it. Two huge boulders were butted up to each other before him at the side of the trail. Behind them rose a hillock with smaller rocks scattered across it, dating from prehistory and now mixed with trees. It looked normal enough. But Hoffmann felt his neck prickle, and he dismounted and tied Jess to a scraggy bush that had grown between the two large boulders.

Suddenly the unmistakable bark of a Winchester rifle close by shattered the silence, and a red-hot slug singed the tasselled shoulder of his buckskin jacket as he dived instinctively for cover below one of the boulders. *That fella couldn't have missed me!* Jess had reared up in fear and had pulled the reins free from the bush. Under cover of the second boulder Hoffman managed to catch her, calm her down and retie her to the bush. Quietly he took his Winchester from the saddle holster.

Sudden anger filled him, but this he could always use, and turn it into a killing. Bushwhacking was the worst crime. Horse stealing and bushwhacking were hanging offences. But was this a warning shot only? He rubbed his shoulder. Pain and blood were there, and with cold, reasoned thought he decided to kill.

Slowly Hoffmann moved away from the boulders and into the cover of cedar bushes and a few elm trees. The rifleman, he knew, must have thought him dead or badly wounded. Finding a good vantage point behind one of the many rocks, he decided to wait for movement higher up. Ten minutes went slowly by, and at last he saw a tan-coloured Stetson lift from the cover of bushes over to his right, then the face of a woman with scared eyes beneath it. The gunfighter levered a shell into the chamber and took careful aim with the Winchester. The woman had tried to kill him – bushwhack him. That was the worse of crimes, justifying a killing. You want to fight like a man, then die like one. The killing position was sure as Jack Hoffmann began to squeeze the trigger.

But instead of sensing danger and moving back into cover, the girl stayed where she was. And this saved her life. It gave Hoffmann the chance to think that this was a *woman* he was about to kill. He lifted his aim instinctively and put a slug right through that tan Stetson. A high-pitched scream rent the air, and as the girl ran for her horse, Hoffmann knew why he had avoided killing. Once again he had managed to contain his anger, which always fired his combat skills, and he now knew that the woman's hurried flight on her horse across the surrounding sea of open prairie would show him where she was going, and almost certainly where she had come from.

***

Eighty miles away Jacob Moses was chopping wood outside his log cabin, which fronted the small farm he had owned in partnership with his now late brother,

Patrick. Together they had worked hard, growing barley, wheat, beans and corn at little more than subsistence level. Nearly a month had passed since Jacob had killed Mal Quincy in the gunfight outside the Midnight Star in Hardin's Bluff. Quincy had killed his young brother on a whim, and Jacob Moses had wanted, and got his revenge. Jack Hoffmann had told Moses that the killing was lawful since it was self-defence and this would spare him from the hangman. But he now had a reputation as a gunfighter, and if he continued carrying a gun, someone quicker would soon come along and take his rep from him. Hoffmann had made good sense, and Jacob had sold his gun-rig and settled to the quiet, hard life he knew as a farmer.

Now a stranger was appearing on an appaloosa horse. Jacob settled himself down on the chopping block as the man rode up; he took out a small, dark cheroot, lit it up, and waited to offer Western hospitality, which was the custom.

Joshua Petersen was tall in the saddle. There was something menacing about him as came up the short incline. He wore a full Mexican-style moustache, the hard features of his face half hidden in shade under a black Stetson, from under which his diamond-sharp blue eyes flickered cautiously around. 'You on your own? 'Cos I've got some good business to offer ya. Don't want no one about ta hear us, ya see?'

Jacob Moses was sweating a little under the hot sun and from the exercise. He looked about. The two men he employed were hard at work repairing fences.

'No one here but me, stranger.'

'The name's Petersen, Joshua Petersen.' He pulled out his half-brother Mordecai's bundle of stolen dollar bills from the stagecoach hold-up, and threw them down on the ground dramatically. 'It's yours, friend. I knows who you are, Jacob. You've now got a powerful reputation as a gunfighter, 'cos you out-drew and killed Mal Quincy – even called him a coward before dispatching him, so's I hear!'

Jacob Moses got to his feet slowly and said nothing. Fear was suddenly in his heart.

'All I want is yourn rep, friend. And I'm willing to pay handsomely fer it. You get my drift? Listen up, I knows that Hoffmann's given you good advice – and you've taken it. Clever boy. You want rid o' that rep, and I'm just the fellow to help yer – and pay yer for it, too!'

The young farmer said nothing. He just stood there, expressionless.

'If'n you accepts my offer and takes this here bundle o' dollars, you'll have farming money ta spend and be able ta keep free o' the gunfighter reputation. Just tell folks the story I'm about ta tell yer, so's they know I'm the man who out-drew you!'

The appaloosa snorted and shied away as two jays flew across the yard, but Petersen reined in the horse and turned back towards Jacob Moses. 'What I wants yer to say is that a man turned up out of nowhere, said his name was Joshua Petersen. He remained sitting on his horse with a six-gun on his hip. Say he demanded that you put on your gun-rig, and challenged you to a fast draw. People will understand that you had no choice when you say this. I knows you done sold your rig in town, but that's another matter. Say you bought a new gun if necessary. Say that Petersen beat you to the draw – make that quite clear – but only grazed the side of your head. Say he then rode off like the wind because he thought you waz dead, 'cos you waz lying on the ground.'

Joshua Petersen smiled evilly. 'That's how you'll earn that there bundle of dollars. You must never reveal the truth, so you can become the rancher who never uses a gun now, as you wants ta be.'

Jacob Moses, for all his bravely standing up against the gunfighter outside the Midnight Star, was a seriously honest man. He was sure that the bundle of dollars before his feet was stolen money. He guessed that it couldn't be traced, and that it could set him up well on the farm. But he had a powerful conscience – a conscience that said he must behave in an honest way.

'I don't want that money, Mr Petersen. I don't want anything to do with your offer. Now get off my land.'

Joshua Petersen hadn't expected that. His half-brother's words had been so convincing. He was momentarily lost, but knew the chance wouldn't come again and that he needed that rep. The man standing there before him stood in his way to untold wealth out in California through gold. Suddenly he drew his six-gun and fired one shot, which drilled a hole through Jacob's forehead. The farmer was blown back by the force of it, turning as he fell on his own brain matter spread across the ground. The two jays, frightened by the gunfire, disappeared over the farmhouse. Joshua Petersen picked up the bundle of dollars and put it in his waistcoat pocket, climbed back into leather and spurred his horse cruelly on its flanks, and galloped away across the wild range.

FIVE

Exactly two weeks later, Kate Strong had a bad night's sleep for the first time in many years. Yes, she would worry when her lover Jack Hoffmann was away, but she had learned to live with it. There was no point in doing anything else, and she had the Midnight Star to run. But this time it was very different. The telegraph message that had been picked up by her cousin, Paddy Flynn, then sent on to her, told of the proposed heist of the gold shipment bound for the Lusk railhead. She had told Jack Hoffmann, accepting that he would take the chance of earning a great deal of bounty money if the gold robbery could be stopped. Both were reasonably happy about it. That particular night Kate could see the heavy wagon in her dreams, its trooper militia riding guard all around as it slowly rumbled along the dirt road. The date in her head was as clear as daylight: 15 July. She tried to put the strange dream out of her mind for days, but it wouldn't go, even with the mighty distractions the Midnight Star brought on. She wanted to share this strange experience with Jack Hoffmann for some unaccountable reason, but there was no way she could.

Kate Strong's home was built at the back of the Midnight Star. It had started out in humbler circumstances as a clapboard rental in Hardin's Bluff. Shrewdness, hard work and good-natured toughness had helped her build up the thriving business from nothing. She had grown with it out of the dusty red soil, which only fifteen years before had been open prairie, where bison roamed, and buzzards flew unchallenged. A rough, tough place set at the very edge of civilization, far out in Wyoming Territory.

Kate had great warmth, but little true respect for men in general, treating them all as spoilt children to be placated – with the exception of one man: Jack Hoffmann. Indeed, as far as it was possible for a woman like her to know love, she loved him. He had been sheriff of Pine Ridge before they met up. A good sheriff, too, until his sweetheart was gunned down by bank robbers. The lawman then suddenly became a law unto himself and set out to kill each member of the gang, one by one. This he did with remorseless efficiency, and then collected the bounty outstanding on three of them. Afterwards, Hoffman took to the hills, prairie and rough-neck towns of the Old West, in search of his quarry – bad men for whom the United States judiciary had placed a bounty – bring 'em in dead or alive was the call – and he did. Facts had grown to legend about the bounty hunter who carried a Colt and a shortened scattergun on his hip, and the West now knew his name from Utah to the Dakotas.

Kate and Jack were two of a kind. She no more wanted to settle down in marriage than he did. But they needed each other a great deal, like winter needs spring. For Kate, the gunfighter was an anchor in rough, unpredictable times. Jack Hoffmann was the only man she had ever been able to trust, for he really did not want or need her money. A house, business and responsibilities were anathema to him, a great burden that he had felt unable to carry since the death of Mary Jane. And it was only that preacher's daughter in Pine Ridge who could have settled him down. Now she was buried in the cemetery there. When Hoffman was tired after months loose in the saddle, or a bounty was paid, or he needed to stay somewhere to rest up a while, only Kate's beautiful body gave him solace and her own spirit replenished his once more. They replenished each other.

***

The Double D ranch business venture, far out in Wyoming Territory, had prospered well. It was here that Jack Hoffmann was heading to meet up with his brother, Shane, and the Longhorn committee, before travelling on to make an attempt to stop the gold heist and win some bounty for himself. Double

D had been set up by Micky Dobson's father, Ben. Ben was killed by a rogue steer when Micky was fifteen. The boy was a game lad. With the help of his father's friends they kept the ranch going and Micky proved to be his father's son when at twenty-two years of age he led a team of five cowboys driving a herd of four thousand longhorn beeves to cattle pens at the railhead in Lusk, Wyoming, for shipment out east. This made his name among cowboys, prairie drifters and townsfolk alike far and wide. Micky was known as being straight, clever and tough. No one messed with him.

The McCormack gang was something else. They were clever too, but bad. They had already robbed three newly developing towns across the wilderness frontier of the Wild West, not by six-gun, but by the fountain pen. Now they were intent on the new township of Longhorn. Ezra McCormack, the gang's undoubted leader, was well aware of Micky Dobson. But he thought he had the measure of him – at least for the few months he needed to fleece Longhorn town dry, before moving on.

Double D ranch house was half lumber and half stone. Inside, a huge fireplace held a roaring log fire even though it was early summer, giving a warm welcome to the soon-to-be-expected guests. At twenty-two, going on twenty-three, Micky Dobson's house had no feminine touches, seeing as he was still single and had no time for ritual courting. The walls were awash with trophies and guns from his father's exploits, but Micky was getting close.

The undoubted owner of Double D was around six feet four tall, and he looked older than his years, having a long, thoughtful face. He was clean shaven and prairie brown from a ragged life spent in the open from a young age. Grey eyes bored out at anyone as the tall young man weighed them up shrewdly, yet they gave nothing away. He had shoulders like a Greek god, although Micky Dobson wouldn't have thanked you for the comparison. He was clever, not from good teaching – he spent few years at school – but with a worldly view on people and life that had been carried down from Ben, his dominating father. When Ben was killed, young Micky had risen to the challenge and had gone his own way without parental guidance, his mother having died after giving birth to twins, a boy and a girl, both of whom were away now at a city college, having inherited their mother's love of learning.

Micky Dobson looked out of the windows at a small cloud of rising dust. His first guest was approaching. It was a man's world outside that ranch house, and inside this one as well. This was the way the young businessman liked it. Duck and dive when necessary, survival is the name of the game. *I am Micky, not Ben Dobson. You had better remember that if you want to continue working for the Double D and for me.* These words were often heard when older men were around Micky, once he had reached eighteen. No one questioned it.

The entrance had a wooden arch with the traditional pair of beef horns above, and under it drove

Luke Schwab in a neat little two-wheel buggy with his wife Maude next to him on the wooden seat. He was sporting a white Stetson hat and a smart business suit from back east when he had lived there. Schwab was the town's solicitor, lawyer and book keeper all joined into one, seeing as he was the only person so qualified in the area. He pulled up outside the ranch house and helped Maude out in her long, flowered summer dress. Soon five other riders followed and tied their horses to the hitching rail. Everyone was in their best clothes, having come from church on this Sunday morn. Micky Dobson stepped out on to the stoop, welcomed his guests and ushered them into the spacious long meeting room with anticipation. Now perhaps a committee could be formed to deal with the McCormack ruffians once and for all.

The gathering of the four ranchers who had spreads around Longhorn town, and two shop owners began smoothly, as easy as any family business group could be; beers and coffees were being enjoyed happily, when Shane Harris arrived with the promised gun-fighter Jack Hoffmann – a killer for hire. Apart from being a meeting to create the town's first committee, this was a gathering of kin: the Harrises, the Dobsons, the Kidmans and the Waterfords. Many families with connections in those parts were bonded together across the open prairie-lands, bonded by their common blood and the need for survival.

But the objective of the meeting was beginning to set minds to the task ahead: the McCormack gang

had to be stopped. Some were in that room as owners of various successful establishments, others of
the far-flung family were not there, less ambitious
perhaps, happily working for businesses on their
own account. Everyone knew the occupation of the
others, everyone had that feeling that kin bestows
on a large family – but no one remembered John
Harris. Such was the distance between the ranches,
and the distance to Longhorn for supplies, that it
had allowed John Harris, Shane's older brother, to
fade from the collective family memory. John has
slipped away at seventeen years old when he had
fled Caspin, his own parents now dead, to a life
outside the law, and had taken on the name of Jack
Hoffmann.

Shane entered the ranch house to Micky Dobson's
welcome and introduced the gunsel, as many in
those parts called him. The talk in the long room fell
to silence as the two men entered. Jack Hoffmann
walked across the boarded floor and stepped on to
an expensive rug at the centre of the gathering with
easy, animal-like movement and a casual ease that
the committee members of Longhorn had never
before seen in anyone close to, an ease that belied
his deadly speed in combat. The stranger was tall,
slim, about six feet one. Although eight in number, including Shane Harris and Micky Dobson,
every man there was hard pushed to keep looking
Hoffmann directly in the eye. His shadowy eyes were
slits in the bright sunlight of a waning, early summer

sun that filtered through the large windows. Long, jet black hair hid none of the gunfighter's face, which had death written into every part. There was a worldly appearance to the man who knew his worth, and it showed quite clearly. Tall and dark. Dark man with dark eyes. The sort of eyes that could look right through you.

Jack Hoffman threw the tan Stetson hat of his recent assailant on the table among schooners of beer and coffee mugs. 'Any of you gentlemen know who owns this here hat?'

Marcus Davis picked it up carefully and pushed a finger through the bullet hole. 'They done had a fight with you, Mr Hoffmann?'

The reply came back cold and straight; a deep voice with the richness of black molasses and an edge to it that made a man shiver. 'That varmint tried to bushwhack me just before Drylake and rode away like the wind afterwards in this direction.'

The hat was handed around to everyone. No one knew who it belonged to.

Hoffmann turned to Micky Dobson who coughed politely. 'Sorry we can't help, Mr Hoffmann,' he said assertively 'It's just like any other you'd find in these parts. Sounds like someone wanted you dead before you got here?'

Hoffmann nodded. 'Pretty sure it was a gal.'

Shock filled the room. The mutter of voices died.

'Spunky gal at that. Caught sight of her eyes briefly. She looked scared.'

Silence fell and Dobson turned to the gathering. 'Gentlemen, let's move across to my guests' table where two o' my boys and Mrs Schwab, who has kindly agreed to help, will bring us drinks – red eye or coffee as the mood takes us. Then we'll get down to some real talking.'

SIX

Eight men settled themselves around Micky Dobson's large polished country table with room to spare. Micky was at the head, Jack Hoffmann at the other end, the remaining six sitting three either side.

'First let us all introduce ourselves,' he growled, nodding at Luke Schwab. 'Will you start, Luke?' The middle-aged man with a sunny smile and healthy complexion nodded.

'Name's Luke Schwab. What th' Good Lord left outa me in body he made up for in brains. Not saying I'm worldly clever, although I'm not stupid either, I've been college taught back East and learned the law's ways well. I've come out West for betterment and been settled here for nearly two years come this fall. Soon as I saw what Ezra McCormack was up to I went to see him at the bank. Hank Munro disappeared some months ago, he was our bank manager – never found out what happened to him – now we got McCormack. He was putting up the mortgage repayments on every business and house in and around Longhorn to twenty-five per cent. That's totally illegal. The critta just sat back in his chair and said to me he knew all about that, and tried to bring me into the swindle, make me a junior partner. When I said no, he just smiled, smug like, and said, "What yer gonna do about it, there ain't no Law around these here parts for 150 miles?" Then all of a sudden the door opens and three of his thugs, including McCormack's newly installed Sheriff Henderson, walk in. They threw me out on the dirt street with an open threat not to visit again ever.'

After a brief, heavy silence, Micky Dobson suggested again that everyone introduced themselves to Mr Hoffmann. The Kane cousins spoke up first to say they were Peter and Ernest and ran the Lazy K spread. Little Tommy Waterford explained how he owned and ran the corn chandlers and the dry goods store across the street to it, and how the twenty-five per cent increase on his mortgage repayments, plus another twenty-five per cent levied on shops in town, would soon have him out of business.

Mark Kidman said he owned Sixty Acre Farm with his kin and could see no hope for the future if the hoodlums were not stopped. Jim Saule explained how he owned the Big S ranch with his sister, after his pa had reached the ripe old age of seventy-eight and passed the ownership on to his two children – all done proper like, with Mr Schwab drawing up the documents. He then said that all his pa, himself and his sister had built up was not going to be taken from them by robbers. He would die first, adding that in another six months the Big S ranch would also be finished because of the gang. He then suggested that they all go in and shoot the lot. This got a cheer of support.

Shane Harris explained that he worked for Peter and Ernest Kane at the Lazy K, and had no interest in business. Shane felt huge relief that no one had made a family link to Jack Hoffmann sitting only a few feet from away from him. Then everyone fell silent. Coffee was poured from another steaming pot that Mrs Schwab brought in, serving the guests politely while they all sat awaiting something to happen. Micky Dobson broke the silence once more.

'This here is my ranch house, my range land outside – it runs as far as the eye can see from here. They are my cattle, three to four thousand head. This here committee is headed up by me. My father started up Double D just before the war between the North and the South, but he died when I was fifteen. I want you to understand that I have made this ranch what it is today, Mr Hoffmann. That is the way of things here. Your presence is welcome and needed. We need your expertise.' He looked to the other end of the long table: two strong men stared at each other. Dobson, for all his bravery, felt the edge of fear.

'Obliged to yuh, Mr Dobson. Plain talking is my way, too,' said the gunfighter. 'I respect honest dealings, sir.' He looked at the others, one at a time, and his stare hung for moments on each man, 'I don't like killing folks, but I do what's got to be done, and I always sleep nights.' He sipped the red eye set before him. 'Always…' The silence was palpable. 'If I may, Mr Dobson, I'd like to make some observations that might help to bring this business at your town to a swift conclusion.'

Micky Dobson nodded, his weather-beaten, handsome face showing no emotion. 'Go ahead, Mr Hoffmann.'

The big man lifted a small gold case from his shirt pocket, took out a cheroot, struck a match on the heel of his boot and lit up the smoke. 'I've come across this town heist before. It only works on a frontier town for a short time when the law has not reached it. Usually the deeds of a property, be it a ranch or shop business, are held by the bank. The first thing to happen is the bank manager and any staff disappear. Being small there is normally only the manager. Then a new one arrives. Changes are made to the mortgage payments, which are substantially increased!'

Everyone agreed and echoed the words. Micky Dobson said that this was what had happened to them all.

'That original mortgage sum is fixed by the first agreement,' Hoffmann continued, 'it cannot be increased. The way these crittas work is that of the bully. If the increased mortgage repayments are not met, then the business reverts to the bank because they hold the deeds. They then throw the legitimate owner and his family off the land and sell the business on to unsuspecting newcomers and make a huge profit. After a short time, afore they're caught, they move on.

'Until the law comes to Longhorn, the six-gun rules here, and the lynch mob. I stands somewhere in that group. But not lynching anyone who has not stood fair trial. I earn my living by finding the bad-men and bringing them to justice for bounty money, bringing 'em in dead or alive. I'm good at it. That's why I'm still alive. The fact that I'm here pays witness to my reputation: I'm a killer with a code – my own code. Folks believe, on the whole, my way is the best compromise to stand against lawlessness until civi-lization arrives. Sometimes I kill bad men because there's no other way. Those crittas avoid me and I need to go looking for them to earn my pay with bounty or rough justice, 'cos that's what folks under-stand is the only justice available out here in the West.'

He looked around the room with dark, clever eyes, strong without fear, and a face long and hard. 'Guess you must agree with this to have invited me here.' Silence reigned again, every man there wondering about his own morals and realizing that Longhorn town had no real choice, or it would die soon. 'Yes. I'm a hired gun. But I never kill unless I believe it is the only way to clear up a mess. And I kill a lot o' hombres!'

The room remained silent – only Micky Dobson was sipping his coffee, a red eye nearby.

'Seems to me that, on the face of it, this McCormack gang have got you tied up just where they want you. If you send a rider out to the nearest telegraph office with a message for the federal marshal, the rider will be shot afore he gets far from town. Have no doubts, they'll have someone watching the trails away from here night and day. They are that good and determined. Ezra McCormack has done this before, by my hearings. He knows what he's about and has got very rich on it.

'Shane Harris has told me that the new sheriff – this imposter – has built hisself a real strong jail at the back of his office.' The gunfighter pulled on his cheroot, the whole room hanging on his every word, and he looked across the floor bleakly. 'Gotta tell you folks that the best way to stop this would be to round 'em up by surprise, then lock the whole darn bunch in that there jail and call the federal marshal in. But that ain't easy, and it's an option that is no longer open to us. The chances are that the gang is on to us already, if I knows Ezra McCormack's ways of doing things, like I do.' Hoffmann looked around the table, dark eyes burning with suppressed anger for them and their cause, his jaw now set with real determination for his new task.

'Yuh see, that girl who almost killed me out Drylake way rode off in this town's direction. There are few towns in this neck o' the woods, so my guess is she's holed up with the gang. And they knows all about my arrival here, and have been watching you people like hawks. The chances are, they even know we're holding this meeting. How Shane Harris managed to get out of town and find me, I don't know.'

Peter Kane spoke up. 'Thought I saw a light-glint on the way over here, Mr Hoffmann.'

His cousin followed. 'Yeah. Like a spy glass being used. I got good eyes, better than Ernest's,' he grinned, 'and I saw some movement up on Murder Ridge, too.'

Jack Hoffmann sat back and took a long pull on his cheroot. 'On the way over here I saw what looked like some old Indian habitation high up on a ridge.'

There was a murmur of understanding from around the table.

'That'll be the ancient ruins at this end of Murder Ridge, overlooking the town. They say it dates back to before the time of the conquistadors down in Mexico.'

'Well,' said Hoffmann, 'that's where we are going to make our first play!' He shot a glance across to Micky Dobson, who was looking seriously at him. 'If that's OK with you, Mr Dobson.' The deep, black molasses voice had a sobering effect. 'I wish to put my plan to your committee, discuss it as you might say, create it by talk, and if you don't like the ideas just let me know. We'll think again.'

Micky Dobson's neutral face broke into a thin smile. 'That I'll do, Mr Hoffmann.' He paused. 'OK. I'll give you your head on this. Ask my friends here anything you need to know, and I'll consider your suggestions as head o' this here committee.'

Jack Hoffmann got up, walked over to the window deep in thought. Then he turned to the seated men and smiled. 'Which one of you gentlemen has connections with mechanical things – make something up for me?'

Little Tommy Waterford surprised everyone. 'I could make mechanisms up for you, Mr Hoffmann. I have a workshop at the back of my corn chandler's shop. Before I moved out West with my wife – we were both little more than kids – I studied science at a college in Chicago and brought my tools and other things with me on the wagon train, even though I was sore tempted to throw everything away many times, for the journey was very hard – but I never did. What do you want me to make you?'

Hoffman smiled. 'I want a timer that will start an explosion up on Murder Ridge twenty-four hours after we set it up! When I was up country, years ago, I heard tell of a man who set up an explosion by dripping water out of a wooden barrel with a tap on it. The water filled a small bucket on the end of a balance arm. When the arm went down it set off an explosion. The fella didn't get away with it, even though he was miles away when the explosion came, an' they hung him in Billings, Montana, a few years back.'

Everyone around the table began talking at once. Micky Dobson raised his voice and brought the committee back to silence with the sharp words, 'Let Mr Hoffmann finish!'

The big man raised his hand in acknowledgement. 'Thank you, Mr Dobson. I noticed, and I expect you are all aware of the overhang of rock beyond this ancient Indian settlement.' He glanced up to Tommy Waterford, who seemed deep in thought. 'Whilst Mr Waterford is musing on the idea of bringing down that rock overhang on open land just before the entrance to your town, I will ask a question of you all. Does the McCormack gang ever meet up in one place?'

'That's a difficult one,' replied Micky Dobson. 'Yer see, those bad men are all over town, anytime o' day, scaring the honest folks witless with threats – even bullying old Mrs Cheesman into giving the gang free meals in her little cook rooms down by the church.'

'Yeah, but they get together after they've had their fill in Sheriff Henderson's office for a bottle or two, some red eye and smokes every lunchtime,' suggested Shane Harris. 'It's only then that the townsfolk kin settle for a few hours in peace.'

'Every lunchtime?'

'Mostly, Mr Hoffman. In fact, that lunchtime meeting is about the only reliable thing about Ezra McCormack and his gang.'

'Mr Hoffmann…' Little Tommy Waterford was all smiles. 'I've had a think about this, and I believe we could do what you say. I don't know much about explosives, dynamite and the like, but I can make you a timer based on the water idea you outlined. It's sure to work, because Archimedes said so.'

'Archie who?' said a newcomer loudly who entered the room in a rush.

'This is Cactus Jim Bowry,' interjected Dobson, introducing the dust-caked range rider to Jack Hoffmann.

'Sorry to interrupt the meeting ya all, but I'm a mite late.'

'Noted,' said Micky Dobson with a glare. 'Unbroken horse again, Jim?'

The man, still dressed in Stetson, check shirt, pants and chaparajos, was banging himself all over among clouds of range dust. 'Yeah. Caught the son o' a bitch though. Finished the breaking in out on the range and rode him back bareback! He won't cause me no trouble again!'

Micky pulled up a chair to the table for the tough-looking man and poured some red eye. 'Jim's got a successful business breaking in mustangs, some found off the range wild, some brought in special like. He even gives riding lessons to those folks who need them.'

Good-hearted laughter crossed the table.

'Like I was saying,' began Little Tommy Waterford, 'Archimedes was the first Greek to start the science of mechanics. He discovered the laws of levers and pulleys and the like.'

'You studied under him?' said a voice.

Tommy glared. 'No, he's dead.'

'What did he die of? A pulley fall on him?'

Laughter.

'A fella beat him with a lever 'cos he was becoming too boring.'

More laughter.

Tommy gave up. 'All I'll say is that if Mr Hoffmann wants this here timer making, I'm the fella to do it

– and…' he smiled at the gathering '…I wants full recognition for this ability to help my business grow! I can make all sorts.'

Jack Hoffmann was looking out of the large ranch-house window again. He turned. 'The way I sees it, we need to take a wagon up to Murder Ridge that won't cause any suspicions from the McCormack gang. Any suggestion?'

'I can answer that!' Jim Saule leaned forwards. 'Old Mrs Cheesman, the widda woman, goes up to the Indian place for water. There's a spring up there, serves the pond. It's always clean drinking water and she brings barrels of it back for her cook rooms. She'll even sell ya some, to save ya riding up there yoursel. That old woman is as strong as a horse! There are two wells in Longhorn town, but the water is rather dirty and they say it's best boiled. No one does, though. Everyone seems to have gotten used to it by now. But Mrs Cheesman's is best.'

Hoffman nodded. 'That's just dandy. Sounds like you can do the timer for me, Tommy. We need a barrel on a stand with a tap on it. Water can come out of the pond, so we can fill the barrel easy. Under the tap on the barrel we fits a bucket on a long arm with a weight at the other end to keep the bucket up. Above the weight is fixed a scatter-gun shell. When the bucket gets near to full with water, the arm goes down and the force of the rising arm at the other end sets the shell off, lighting a fuse to the explosive.' He smiled in the silence. 'How long for you to make it, Tommy?'

Little Tommy Waterford grinned. He wanted to prove himself. 'Two days at the most. I can't supply the dynamite or whatever though.'

'There's no worry with that! I got more than enough stored from the days of the old mine.' Jim Saule nodded. 'Keep it dry. Keep it clean. Ya never knows when it might come in handy!'

SEVEN

The ancient Indian dwelling, maybe over a hundred years old, was single storey and made of adobe bricks. It was run down, but the new arrivals up on Murder Ridge could see how the original builders had grown crops up there, drawn water from the pond out the back – which held clean water fed by a spring – and had managed a primitive sort of living. The building was a good distance away from the drop, so a long fuse would be necessary if they were to set up the timer in the building.

Tommy Waterford, who was slight of build but strong, found an animal track that let him put Jim Saule's dynamite under the overhang, where he buried it into soft earth, noting to the others that it wouldn't take much to bring everything down. Jack Hoffmann insisted that a lot of dynamite be used, because the idea was to bring everyone in town outside, including McCormack and top men of his gang who were due to carouse after their midday meal in the newly constructed sheriff's office. The problem was that the water timer could not be relied upon to work within an hour of setting. So they would have to work with that. It didn't take long for the basis of the mechanism to be set up – Little Tommy was everywhere and doing everything. Then with the team well back from the drop and out of sight in the frontier town below them, Jack Hoffmann got them all to sit on the dirt floor in one of the rooms.

'I want to explain mah plan to you folks. If we are lucky and the explosion goes off when we want it to, and McCormack and his close buddies are taking it easy after their midday meal, having a siesta , that's one thing to our advantage – then I'll go in and make a citizen's arrest!' He laughed bitterly, 'Could cause a bit o' bother and I'd have to kill a few of them. But we can't rely on that explosion time. So we need a plan that will take account o' that. This means I'll need help; first thinking was some of yuh who are handy with guns…' There was a scrabble of voices all keen to help. The gunfighter raised his hand. 'Thanks for this. The problem is, should things go wrong – and they could – McCormack and his gang would recognize the men who tried to stand against him. I don't need to tell yuh all what that would mean. I just need is one good man to help me. It'll be enough. Someone the gang don't know too well. Someone who lives outa town, outa the normal ranch spread places. Someone who spends his time near the open range and don't come into Longhorn much.'

'Thats gotta be me.'

They all turned to Cactus Jim Bowry.

Jack Hoffmann smiled, a rare open smile and pushed his black Stetson hat back on his head. 'Well Jim, you took the words right outa mah mouth.'

There was that sudden, strange atmosphere across the gathering where everyone wanted to laugh and no one did. This was too important.

'You sure?'

'Certain. How do you think I got my moniker?'

Hoffmann gave a thin smile. 'Dunno.'

'When I was ten years a pony I was riding threw me into a cactus patch. I hit some, broke one or two in pieces, and got spikes all over. Climbed outa the patch, and got more spikes in getting' out. The pony ran off and I walked two miles back to my pa – Ma being dead – leaving a trail of blood all the way behind me. I never did learn to quit.'

Silence.

'You can use guns?'

'Got a Winchester carbine, two Colt Peacemakers, plus a Navy Colt. The Peacemakers on both hips, the Winchester in my hand ifn I really mean business. Five years ago two men tried to take over my horse-breaking business by force. They didn't come back. I can use guns all right when needs drive. And they drive mightily now!'

***

Just as dawn was rising two days later, the timer still in its final construction stage, Jack Hoffmann rode into

Longhorn town with a gunny sack tied to the cantle. He approached the new sheriff's office, rebuilt from Widow Peggity's rooming house, the large front window still there. The sheriff's desk was behind the window, so he could watch the street outside. All was silent. All was empty. It was dawn. Hoffmann took the gunny sack from the cantle and gently spurred Jess into a gallop, whirring the sack around his head and released it perfectly to smash through the window and land on Sheriff Henderson's desk. The gunny sack contained some rocks, ripe horse manure to offend, and a note stitched to the outside to say that Jack Hoffmann was coming into town that day and would be calling out the Coyote Kid from the Buffalo Saloon on Main. He wanted to bring him in, dead or alive, for the bounty.

Hoffmann knew this would open up a hornet's nest. They would sweat on those hours of waiting, nervously setting their trap. Riflemen up on rooftops. Others at windows or behind water butts and the like in the streets. He was gambling on the fact that he wouldn't be killed on his way in, because McCormack would want to see the play between him and his hired gun, the Coyote Kid, outside the Buffalo Saloon. Two reasons for this. The first was to see if his hireling was as good as he was supposed to be, the second was that all bad men in the West wanted to see who killed Jack Hoffmann in a fair fight. By now the name of Jack Hoffmann had spread that far. Ezra McCormack could only gain from this and would not want to miss the opportunity of being the one who had more or less arranged the whole thing.

Jack Hoffmann and Cactus Jim Bowry talked on this point at some length. Jim had a cousin called Jake Dobson – close kin to Micky Dobson as it happened, who had a three-storey clapboard house near the entrance to Longhorn town. He knew that Jake would be only too keen to help. He told the gunfighter that an upstairs room in Jake's house had a wide view over town. As Hoffmann rode in to confront the Coyote Kid, Jake Dobson would sight up his rifle on the first gunman he saw covering Hoffmann. Should the man look like he would shoot, Jake would shoot first. And that rifle crack would be the signal for Hoffmann to turn and make a quick getaway. It was good insurance, just in case.

Getting out afterwards, that was the real problem. Hoffmann wasn't afraid of facing the Kid, he had taken men like him before, and Jack Hoffmann was a clever tactician. He knew the odds on Jess outrunning so many hostile guns from the middle of town would be pushing his luck much too far. So together with Cactus Jim, who proved to be as devious as necessary for the task, they hatched the main plan. Some of the others on the committee suggested a route down an alley opposite the Buffalo Saloon that a man on a galloping horse could take. What was more, they realized that there was the danger of an upstairs room being available in a house opposite the Buffalo Saloon where a member of the McCormack's gang could be

76

ready in wait with his rifle, should Hoffmann win the draw with the Coyote Kid.

Cactus Jim picked up on this point. He would position himself in the alley the committee had suggested before Jack arrived. If he outdrew the Kid, Jim would already have the gunman at the window in his sights, aimed and ready. The report from Jim's rifle would let Hoffmann know the direction he was to take, his horse tied to a hitching rail nearby for the quickest getaway. Anyone of the gang who followed would be taken out by Jim Bowry as they followed Jack, and together with Jim, the two men would destroy a large number of McCormack's gang as they tried to follow, then scoot as soon as they were able. A picket fence would need to be cleared afterwards, but that was all that could stop them getting clean away.

If the ploy was successful, there would be only McCormack and his close henchmen to deal with later, using the distraction of the explosion up on Murder Ridge to draw them out of the sheriff's office in complete surprise.

***

Cactus Jim Bowry rode out of Micky Dobson's ranch beside Jack Hoffmann just before dawn. It was almost pitch black, the sun's rays just appearing like fingers of gold through a distant treeline. They had left directly on to open range away from the town's entrance so that their departure could not be noted by friend or foe alike. Jack Hoffman, ever the cool-minded tactician, was going to take a circuitous route back into town so that he would enter for the show-down gunfight with the Kid by late afternoon. Not too late for daylight to be at its best, high summer was all around, but long enough for the McCormack gang to sweat – particularly the Coyote Kid. At just after 7am, Jim Bowry and Jack Hoffmann took their different routes and went their own ways. Jim was to return to friends who had a small farm on the edge of town – such was the early development of Longhorn as a frontier town that the farm and its buildings were less than a mile from the Buffalo Saloon at its centre. A wonderful bolthole for Jack and Jim after the gun-fight should it go as planned.

As he rode on to higher ground, the erstwhile run-away of seventeen years and now proven gunfighter and successful bounty hunter, reined his horse to a gentle stop. He was ever the loner; that was how Jack Hoffmann – once John Harris – had survived, and by Western standards had prospered. He thought of Hickok's teaching and Wyatt's, and knew his time was limited. No matter how good a man was, he could not out-draw every badman in the West for ever. Jack determined on using this wonderful gift of speed and agility to destroy evil whenever he confronted it, and hoped that this would last long enough for the laws of Congress to reach these frontiers, and he could put down his burden forever.

Longhorn was the town of his kin; they had helped to build it. No one there knew that the gunfighter was family, their own kith and kin. He liked it that way, kin folks were an unnecessary burden; yet he felt a family connection to so many people of his own blood now living in Longhorn and clearly needing defence. He must succeed for their sake as well as his own, and as usual, before a dangerous encounter, he let his mind and body relax in the only place he felt totally at ease. He and Jess were now at a long ridge. Before them were the beginnings of vast untouched lands full of forests, chaparral heathlands, rivers, wide open skies that were completely virginal and free.

Hoffmann turned Jess and stopped; sitting completely still, he looked back admiring the scene before him and felt his spirit strengthen. Far away a sea of faint waving grasses fanned out to become part of the great Wyoming plain, which, seen from here, ebbed into skyline castles of white cloud. Hoffmann was slim, over six feet tall, and sat on the horse as if he had grown there. His eyes were slits beneath a low-crowned, black Stetson in the bright, dusty light of a summer sun just past its zenith. Tall and dark. Dark eyes. The sort of eyes that could look right through you. He knew this about himself now, and its effect. He used the advantage well to make men think twice before confronting him.

Jack patted his horse. 'Quiet Jess. Quiet girl.' The animal shook its head gently and nickered, then became as still as its master. Behind him stood grey-blue mountains with elm, oak, cedar and sagebrush on the lower slopes, interspersed with scrub, alfalfa grass and wildflowers at rimrock and hill.

Jack Hoffmann rode on, feeling his body and mind refreshed with the easy journey. He opened a burlap bag and took out some beef jerky, which he ate with a hunk of sourdough bread, checking the sun's travel across the skies as he ate, and then began the descent towards Longhorn.

***

Everything looked as good as it could be, ten hours after he had tossed his loaded gunny sack through the window of the sheriff's office. Jess and her master entered Longhorn by the bullet-riddled sign at an easy pace. They rode into town slowly and carefully, Hoffmann feeling complete and quick. He had prepared well, and knew that one of Cactus Jim Bowry's kin was sitting high up in his three-storey house on guard somewhere. He didn't know where, only that the man had a carbine at the ready, to take out any of the gang who might be trigger happy.

The gunfighter was riding his hunch to the limit: to take a bullet in the back would mean the unseen assailant's certain death, because it would mean that he had broken McCormack's order to let Hoffmann ride unmolested into town and dismount outside the Buffalo Saloon. The gunfighter was easy in the saddle, not phased or scared, for he knew his strengths – and looked up to see a rifleman on the roof of a clapboard building pointing a Winchester straight at him.

Suddenly the man withdrew his weapon, unaware that this movement had just saved his life. Jake Dobson did not know for sure if the gunman was about to fire, but his instruction was to warn Hoffmann so that he could turn tail and get out. But Dobson's shot wasn't necessary, and Hoffmann's hunch was right. The bad men were going to let him in, right up to the Buffalo Saloon.

Jake Dobson got to his feet and stepped out on to a recently finished veranda, legs apart, his prized '73 Winchester cradled in brawny arms, staring after the gunfighter. Hoffmann rode on, sensing the town's ill-at-ease, hair-trigger setting. He looked across to a hotel: someone was staring out of the long window, but they quickly looked away; he rode on past a builder's yard rich with smells of tar and lumber, an old man asleep up on the stoop in a rocking chair. The gunfighter's awareness of everything surrounding him was total: he noted the old man open one eye, then shut it. He was not asleep.

Past a livery and corral, horses frisky and whinnying, as if they could sense something too; on past a Lands Office agent where dreams abounded of getting a rail spur into town from the mainline of the Union Pacific railroad one day; then past a blacksmith's forge, a muscular man stripped to the waist working hard in the bright glow of his hearth, the ringing of hammer blows skilfully striking and bouncing off red-hot steel. Hoffmann realized that work had to go on, contracts had to be met for the honest and decent people there. It was only the McCormack gang who had the luxury to wait and sweat out their future. The dirt road now had a boardwalk, with hitching rails. The main street was wide with two blocks on either side for businesses and houses, many yet to be built. This town was laid out with a plan for growth.

He rode on past a feed and grain store, a gun-smith's shop with hardware displayed in the window – a man in a long grey slicker watched his approach but turned away quickly, looking intently in the gun-shop window now; past a turning with a high board that said Kimberley Street; an assay office, a barbering parlour, a harness-maker, a dry-goods and an empty shop that was having a window put in. As Hoffmann approached, the two men positioned the glass against a clapboard wall and moved inside quickly. He saw all this at one glance as he rode. The gunfighter remem-bered everything – clearly. That was part of his skill and why he still lived.

Sounds grew of gaiety, laughter and a hard-played tinny piano. Ahead loomed a square with young saplings set in neat rows at its perimeter, and at the far end stood the Buffalo Saloon. It was typical of saloons across the length and breadth of the West, and Hoffmann was at ease with what he saw. The Buffalo consisted of a two-storey, wood-frame build-ing. Inside, a railed walkway ran round the upper level of the saloon where women little more than tarts and prostitutes took customers for a ride, often in both senses of the word. Many lamps hung from the underside of the upper floor for effect which the gunfighter could see through windows curtained at the corners as he approached.

The bright noise was broken at sporadic intervals by the shouts of drunken men and the sudden crash of what sounded like a brawl. Someone was screaming orders and obscenities. Suddenly the air was thick with foul taunts and insults: such marauding came out of nowhere, so that friend was thumping friend, and chairs were being used as weapons in a quickly growing fury. A woman screamed, a piano started up again with a new tune meant to soothe the quickly changing scene.

Beyond this wildness and carousing, the oasis of stilled quietness in the town outside appeared almost desolate and depressingly quiet by comparison. Jack Hoffmann's eyes still roamed all around on guard. The bulky false-front façade of the saloon thrusting its wooden shoulders high revealed something else: up there, for a split second, he caught the glimpse of dangerous movement.

Still astride Jess, his darkling eyes turned immediately to the building opposite. There was indeed a man high up at the window with a rifle, just as he had been warned. The man moved away quickly, but not quick enough for Hoffmann to register it. The building's squat, threatening dominance over the town's square, which had been laid out with much care for a prosperous future, seemed dirtied by its presence. The wind arose a little, lifting trampled dust to surround a line of tethered horses near its front. Above

the batwing doors a sign read, *Beer, Girls and Cards.*
Jack Hoffmann saw all and was ready.

He dismounted slowly and carefully, tied Jess to
a hitching post so that he could release her in a
split second, and walked slowly and deliberately
towards the batwings. As he walked the noise of
revelry began to abate, then died to nothing in seconds as he heard a guttural man's voice shouting for
silence. Everything fell away, just the ringing of his
silver spurs on the dirt hard street. As he drew near,
false sheriff Henderson came out and stood on some
steps. Everyone inside was crowded at the windows
now, watching.

'We don't want no fighting in this here town.' His
grin was large and almost obscene.

Hoffmann stood before him, large, impressive and
cool. Feet apart. 'I've come to call out the Coyote
Kid…'

Behind Henderson the batwings creaked and a
man stepped out with long, greasy, shoulder-length
hair. He was hatless, had a thin moustache. In his
early thirties, he was dressed all in black with polished
boots. On his hip was a Colt Peacemaker, oiled and
polished.

'My name's Edwin Curry – know me as the Coyote
Kid, friend.'

You could hear a pin drop, even the wind seemed
to have eased. 'I earn mah living by taking gunmen
in for bounty against their name – dead or alive. I'm
very good at it. Yuh want to come peaceable?'

The batwings creaked again and a man dressed in faded jeans and a chequered shirt – cowboy style – slid by quickly before anything happened. He sported a dark curly beard. It was Ezra McCormack.

Silence reigned for long moments as the Kid weighed things up, then he went for his gun – but Jack Hoffmann was quicker. There was no need for diving across the road, rolling away in the dust to draw old Betsy out. He just watched as one less bully boy dropped slowly to the ground, dispatched with clinical efficiency to his maker. Suddenly a girl no more than twenty years of age threw herself on the bloody body, screamed and turned to Hoffmann.

'You bastard,' she cried out.

Hoffmann recognized those eyes: they belonged to the bushwhacker who had tried to kill him as he first rode towards Longhorn. That's when he thought they were the eyes of a woman.

Three clicks from his Peacemaker as the gunfighter drew the hammer back made the point: he swung his six-shooter around pointing at the crowd and then up to the rifleman at the window who seemed to be in shock. Then he smiled a cold smile. 'That fella sure has a way with womenfolk.'

A youth was standing with his mouth open at the end of the building. 'Hey, you come over here – now!' The boy ran forward as if his life hung on the order, Hoffmann pushed the girl away with no feeling, bent down, turned the blood-soaked body over and pulled a necklace from the gunman's neck with a snap of its fine chain. He knew about the killer from dodgers in and around Goodland county. The Coyote Kid, for all his apparent bravery, was a coward. He had killed the girl who loved him in a fit of temper, yet kept her picture in a clasp around his neck out of sheer bravado.

'OK boy, get that burlap bag off the cantle on mah horse, take this rat's spurs off him and put 'em in the bag.' All the time he was watching the crowd, his Peacemaker cocked and in killing position. And they knew it.

The youth did as he was bid, then Hoffmann dropped the necklace into the bag and the youngster ran over to Jess, tying it back on the cantle. Hoffmann had taken the Kid's spurs and the necklace as proof that he had killed him, because there was a bounty out on Curry as a cold-blooded killer, and bounty hunting was how Hoffmann earned his living.

A loud report sounded from ahead. Hoffmann turned to see the rifleman drop forwards out of the open casement window, the carbine falling to the ground as Hoffmann drew out the scattergun: he held both deadly firearms on the crowd. 'Just looks like you're gonna shoot at me, and ol' Betsy here will get a few of yer in one darned go.' He moved back slow and careful to Jess, who whinnied and snorted, reholstered the scattergun and, fleet of foot, mounted the horse. A sudden hail of bullets came far too close as he ducked and spurred Jess away, but instantly Cactus Jim Bowry returned repeated fire from dead ahead. Crouching low in the saddle, Jack Hoffmann made one of the closest escapes of his life, as bullets passed him in both directions until he was safely in the confines of the alley.

Before the gunfire had ceased, a tall stovepipe hat and the long salubrious face of Longhorn's mortician appeared around the end of the Buffalo Saloon, a tape measure at the ready in his white hand.

EIGHT

Together both men fired their Winchesters at McCormack's gang as they rushed down the street towards them. The firing was relentless, a swirling mist of blue smoke filled the air.

'Got two of them at least.'

Jack nodded. 'I reckon four with me.'

Soon, both men were galloping down the narrow confines of the alley and leaping over the picket fence at the end. They had done it.

Ten minutes later they galloped into the yard of Sixty Acre Farm, where Mark Kidman's younger brother led the horses into a barn and then through to a good clean stable with plenty of fresh straw. Mark Kidman, a big-boned, jolly man with long red hair, a sun-burned bald pate and large darting eyes, led them into his log-walled farmhouse home. Sitting on a home-made, sturdy sofa was Little Tommy Waterford, Mark's cousin, once removed. Little Tommy, so named because he stood no more than five foot in his stocking feet, was not put down by anyone because of his size, for he could fight like a bobcat on fire – as they would say. He jumped up full of excitement. 'Kill any of the gang?'

'Mr Hoffman reckons on four, between us.'

Both men whistled. Mark Kidman bade the two gun-fighters sit down on the sofa, and Tommy happily moved to a country chair by a crackling fire set in the large stone fireplace. Mrs Kidman, a big cheery woman, the equal of her husband in size and personality, brought in schooners of frothy-headed beer and sumptuous vittles on a large tray, putting it all down on an equally sturdy home-made table. Mark had a workshop and could turn his hand to much anything. A large mongrel dog joined the party, settling down on the last part of the sofa next to Jack Hoffmann, who petted it with a large gentle hand. He liked dogs. Many people said he pre-ferred the company of animals to human beings.

They ate and drank their fill in silence, after the events that could well have cost the two fighting men their own lives. A small respite was very welcome, and all the party enjoyed the food and drink; Herby the dog had finished his bowlful too and settled down beside Jack's booted feet in an alert doze.

There remained a quiet ten minutes while every-body regained themselves. Jack Hoffmann then sat forward and looked across to Tommy by the fireplace. 'The timer's set up inside the Indian building up on Murder Ridge then, Tommy?'

'Yes, sir! I've practised in my workshop – it takes about twenty-four hours for the water to fill the bucket to the right level to tip the balance arm. It takes only a small opening of the tap on the water barrel. Made a little gauge to set the tap each time.'

Jack Hoffman nodded. 'Well done. Let's hope it'll only be needed the once. Jim and I have set the gang alight with our escapade today. They've lost the best gunfighter they know of and must be rattled as hell. We need to keep the pressure up.' He looked at a big clock standing in the corner. 'Can you ride up to Murder Ridge now and set the timer up to go off between one and two o'clock tomorrow afternoon?'

Tommy Waterford thought for a moment, then nodded enthusiastically. 'Sure thing, Mr Hoffmann. Can't guarantee it'll fire up the shotgun cartridge an' set the fuse a-going at that time 'zackly, but sure as hell it won't be too far away!' With a courteous touch of his forefinger to everyone in turn, the little man took his Stetson from a stand and was gone.

'Now to the next stage, gentlemen. Jim and me need to be in walking distance o' that sheriff's office just before one o'clock. Got any kin or anyone you knows who could put us up there overnight?'

Mrs Kidman came in. 'What about Aunt Bessie, Mark? She an' Billy Tanner owe you a buck or two for that kitchen table you mended.'

He nodded. 'Ifn she and Billy will give 'em board overnight, we'll call it quits.'

***

Bessie and Billy's wood-framed, white clapboard house was exactly the type that the West had put up as towns grew and settlers moved in. It had a neat little picket fence surrounding it, and a seat for two or three to sit comfortably out front, next to the dirt road. Opposite was what had once been Widow Peggity's rooming house, a large building of the same type as was common in growing towns out across Wyoming Territory. The difference now was that the McCormack gang had, by bullying and threat, bought her out using questionable money from the bank, and sent her and a few of her things on the stage to Laramie. The rooming house was now de facto the Sheriff Henderson's jail and the base for their evil plans.

Cactus Jim Bowry and the bounty hunter sat on Aunt Bessie's seat that evening to get the feel of the area around the sheriff's office and jail, which was fronted on the other side to them so they had some cover from the gang's comings and goings. Even so, Jack insisted that they didn't stay sitting there long in the open. He had got to like Jim Bowry in the short time they had been together.

The horse breaker was a good, tough man. Of average height and build, he had an abundance of thick brown hair over a sun-burned, healthy face. Brawny arms had tattoos of an anchor on each. As they talked, Jim said that he had never been to sea, but thought the tattoos would represent his love of Goodland county and his home town of Longhorn. He was anchored there for life, and if any gunslicks thought they could move him away, like poor Mrs Peggity, they would have another think coming. Mrs Pegitty's husband, who was an experienced tattooist from Chicago way, did the tattoos for a few dollars before he died. Jim had a large smile that beamed out of an agreeable face. He talked easily, though he was very quick to anger – but even so, Jack respected him, and knew he had made a firm friend.

Aunt Bessie proved to be a quiet, diligent lady of late middle years. Billy Tanner was the opposite of being quiet. He showed the two his old Buffalo gun that was, in keeping with the type, single shot. But it was so old, it needed black powder in it. Billy was keen to help Mark's boys, as he called the two strangers, but they declined gently. Even so, it was good to have an old-timer who was still willing to fight.

At just after one o'clock they were all sitting in the back yard in pensive mood when the distant sound of a shotgun sounded. It was the cartridge fired by the timer up on Murder Ridge.

'How long would the fuse take to run down to the overhang?' Jim was alight with excitement.

'Bout thirty seconds. We've gotta move. You position yourself on the right of the jail house, me on the left. Let's go.'

As they ran out of the side door, Jim called out, 'What happens if that damned dynamite don't blow?'

They sprinted across the little lawn and cleared the picket fence together. 'We'll cross that one if it happens!'

At that moment a mighty roar filled the whole town. It seemed to shake the very foundations of the houses all around as the two fighters reached either side of the long jail house. Instinctively they carried on to the front as Ezra McCormack and three henchmen came rushing out of the front door. They all watched spellbound as Murder Ridge overhang continued flying up in the air amid clouds of fire-smoke and debris.

'Get your hands up – all of you!' Hoffmann walked out from the cover at the end of the jail, his Colt .45 in killing position.

The gang turned around, shock written into every face.

'Get your hands real high so's we can see there's no monkey business from you varmints.'

They all turned to Cactus Jim Bowry who was holding his Winchester rifle high.

'I know you. Horse breaker up yonder on the wild range,' said Ezra McCormack with a nasty leer.

'Never seen you in my life. Now you and your buddies are going to jail.'

Hoffmann continued for him. 'This jail house you've built will do fine, perhaps the hanging judge could be brought into Longhorn, he's around these parts so I hear.'

But then they all turned to see a double-barrelled shotgun appear suddenly out of the door opening, and a greasy, evil-looking man who kicked the swinging door back shut with the heel of his boot. 'Just you all stand 'zactly where you are. Holster your hardware now and let Mr McCormack put you all in his jail for disturbing the peace.'

'Well done, Sidney.'

The sound of falling earth and rocks rent the oddly silent air about them.

'What kept you?

The greasy man grinned, showing broken teeth. 'I was just having a shit. Somethin' wrong with those beans.'

He had just finished his sentence when a great crash came through the back window of the jail house, through the front door window in an instant, and a half-inch slug ripped through the man's back, blowing his entrails forwards across the common land outside, and him dead at Ezra McCormack's feet. It took a split second for Jim Bowry to take out a stocky man in dungarees next to McCormack as he went for his gun. A deft hand at his Winchester's magazine lever, a blur of movement, and a perfect shot taken from the waist shook all with its speed. Together Jack Hoffman and Jim Bowry stopped the so-called Sheriff Henderson with double gunfire as Henderson drew his Peacemaker and turned to shoot at them whilst running for his horse, which was rearing and whinnying at the gun fire.

Then Ezra McCormack made his play, all in a moment of time that couldn't be measured. A .45 slug whistled past Jack Hoffmann's head from another who was down on the ground playing dead. Jack dived and rolled across the dirt, pulling Betsy free from the specially made scabbard on his left hip: the boom of it was as loud as it was dramatic, and the man died instantly. Jack was still moving like a mountain lion across the bare earth when another deafening report from Jim's carbine pulled him up directly – then McCormack was crying out in pain holding his wrist, the six-shooter down on the floor, as he turned to see his last henchman blown away by Hoffmann's scattergun.

'Well, we've got to lock someone up, Jack. McCormack's the only one left now. Hope you don't mind me winging him…' He trailed off as Hoffmann got up, his dark burning eyes set at his new partner as he reloaded the smoking scattergun and slid it back in his gun-rig.

McCormack was squealing badly now as Hoffmann yelled, 'Shut it, McCormack, you're going back into your own jail – this time on the other side of the bars.' He picked up his Stetson from the floor, banged and straightened it, then gave Jim Bowry a very long look.

'Like me, Jim, you don't like killing folks unless you really got to…' He grinned suddenly. 'Glad you're a good shot. Muh life must have rested on it!'

The horse breaker looked a little shaken. 'Thanks, Jack.' There was a measure of humility to his words, then he rallied. 'Say, where did that Buffalo gunshot come from?'

'Couldn't resist it.' Billy Tanner came round the end of the building holding Aunt Bessie's hand and the long buffalo gun in the other. 'Danged powerful, that black powder. I put in a mite more than yer should.' He winked. 'Just for luck.'

Then a gunshot sounded not far away.

They all turned to see a tall stovepipe hat and the long salubrious face of Longhorn's mortician appear around the end of a clapboard building in the next street, a tape measure at the ready once more in his white hand. ''Scuse me gentlemen,' he cried, 'but I heard some commotion and thought I might offer my services…'

Suddenly an elderly woman came running around the end of the building, past the mortician and straight towards Jack Hoffmann in floods of tears, her face dirt-streaked, as she desperately clung to his arm.

The gunsmoke had barely blown away on the breeze as the big man held her close. 'What's wrong, Miss Pierce? Don't take on so. Did the explosion frighten you?'

She suddenly pushed herself away from his large chest. 'Takes a lot more'n that ta scare *me*, young man!' Then she clasped on to him again, and cried:

'They've shot my dog, Mr Hoffmann! They broke in through the back with an axe, 'cos I've money hidden under my bed. I took it out of the bank 'cos I didn't trust that new manager fellow. They came for it, I'm sure of that, and when the big bang came up on Murder Ridge, we all rushed outside. One man grabbed hold of me, so Elmer went for him, got hold of his leg and the other, nasty-looking man,' she burst into tears, 'he shot poor Elmer dead.'

Suddenly two riders galloped by as if they were being chased by the Devil himself. There was little chance of getting a shot at them because the suspected robbers were shielded by shops and wood-framed houses, and folks were now everywhere as well, walking about in a daze after the great explosion. The bounty hunter gently took her by the shoulders and turned her to face Bessie and Billy Tanner, saying to them: 'I know you'll take care of her. I need to go now!'

As Jack Hoffmann disappeared around the back of the jail house, Bessie cuddled Miss Pierce gently and said, 'How did you know Mr Hoffmann then, Miss Pierce?'

'Elmer ran up to him. Mr Hoffmann was wearing his guns an' all, but to my surprise he bent down and stroked the dog and picked him up. Most folks don't get the chance to pick Elmer up, he won't have it! We got talking, I gave him my name, Western politeness you understand, and he gave me his. He's a nice man.'

Billy, ever the practical man, suggested they walk round to her house and check if the money was still under the bed.

Jess was hitched near to the Tanners' house, and she snickered as Hoffmann came running up beside her. He patted the big horse, saying 'Good girl, Jess. We've got a bit of riding to do.' In a second he was up into leather and riding full pelt out of town. The dirt road was full of confused townspeople, wagons, carts and buggies. Horses were being ridden towards Murder Ridge, but Jack Hoffmann was riding in the opposite direction, as much by instinct as anything else. At the edge of town he called out to a boy and a youth who were loading lumber on a cart.

'Seen two riders coming this way?'

They turned and nodded. 'That way sir,' the youth pointed. 'Up into yonder wood. Going like the wind.'

Jack Hoffmann thanked them and rode on at speed. He knew Jess well, where she could run and when to ease her speed so she didn't get too tired and could still give of her best. A fine trail led into the wood. He dismounted, knowing the danger this brought, and looked carefully for clues as to the bad-men's passage. His Indian friends over the years had taught him much about tracking – where you could follow and where you couldn't. A trail over an open, much used track or hard-packed dirt roadway was very difficult to follow if traffic there was busy.

He moved carefully into the cover and picked up on small, but clear evidence of a fast passage – twigs that were broken, horses' hooves marking the track that were fresh. He had seen the wood from afar when riding towards Longhorn in the past, and he decided to quietly skirt around the outside. It was unlikely the two robbers were setting up a trap for him inside the wood. They would be too keen on leaving the area. He didn't know where they were heading, so he remounted Jess and sat still thinking things through. There was no point in racing off in the wrong direction.

He walked Jess quietly along the outside of the wood, keeping his eyes and instincts targeted through the trees and fauna. There was no sign of his adversaries. Eventually he reached the other end, where he found the trail leading out and up over a hill that was littered with mesquite and wildflowers.

Hoffmann tied Jesse's reins to the branches of a tree and squatted down on the edge of the wood where the trail left its confines. Soon he had found good evidence of a hurried exit by the horsemen, newly broken twigs and fresh hoofmarks. The gunfighter sat down, his back resting on an oak tree, and lit up a small cheroot. It seemed to help his thinking, calmed him and he looked up at Jess.

'Where do yuh think those varmints have gone, girl?' The horse shook its head and started eating the grass. Jack Hoffmann smiled to himself. He had learned a lot from Indian friends and seasoned homesteaders over the years. He mixed it with his own natural ability for tracking. This sixth-sense mixture had proved powerful and often led the range rider to sensitivities he didn't realize he had – and often saving his life. He pulled together his knowledge of the area. It was often said that Jack Hoffmann never forgot a landscape or a town that he passed through. He had a photographic memory, when photographs were still in their infancy.

The trail led over the hill before him, and joined a bigger trail that could take mule packs and small wagons to and from Longhorn. It ran outwards towards small human gatherings and finished at distant Laramie. Word was that a stagecoach line would soon be running along it. Hoffmann knew that the bad men would only ride away from Longhorn, and so he set off at a good pace. The small trail led over the hill and he was soon on his way towards the first town, Harpersville. He met no one on the road for some miles, and as it drew dark he turned off, making camp near a small stream. He led Jess over to the stream where she drank her fill, then they returned to the shelter of some ash trees where he removed her saddle and settled her down on a mossy place by a bush. He settled himself down under one of the trees, rested his head on the saddle and was quickly in an easy sleep.

The big man rose just after dawn, broke open a pack from the two gunny sacks that had been tied to the cantle and took out cooking utensils. Soon a pan was steaming over the newly started fire, and he added some Arbuckle to the boiling water as Aunt Mimi used to do when he was a boy. Then beans and bacon into a frying pan. Breakfast washed down with lashings of the steaming hot coffee that set him up for the day, and all that must be ahead if he could find the robbers. It was a good meal, the best he had enjoyed for a while. The solitary openness of the wild was the best companion Jack Hoffmann knew, and the only close one he needed right then. He could always sleep nights even if he had been forced to kill that day. This ability kept him sane in a world full of dangers.

Jess snickered a welcome as he approached her after strip-washing in the icy stream. Soon she was tacked up with saddle and equipment, and Hoffmann led her over to the little stream where she drank her fill. The gunfighter swung up into leather once more, reined the horse back towards the trail and gently prodded her flanks.

Luck comes into the life of everyone at times, and after an hour on the trail Jack Hoffmann's sharp eyes spotted grass that had been messed slightly where a horse had left its mark coming off the trail. Soon the rocky track ran down into a gulley. The gunfighter stopped Jess in a moment of ill ease. Nothing was obviously amiss. He could see a large buzzard wheeling overhead and noticed the spoor of an animal close to the track. Nothing really unusual... but... Hoffmann dismounted, took Jess into good cover and slipped across to the other side of the track silently. For a big man he was almost invisible among trees, fauna and rock. He owed much to the Indian friends he had known, and knew it. This ability for stealth now came automatically as he moved – it wasn't a thought-out methodology that a specialist soldier learns. Silent movement was now part of him, and soon he had climbed to higher ground. He worked his way along near the top, just under cover, and heard voices.

'Gone quiet,' said a whispered voice.

'Birds stopped singing. Always a sign,' came the careful reply from the other side of the track.

'Always a sign of somethin'.'

Three clicks from a Peacemaker's hammer being pulled back together with the cold steel of its barrel behind the ear, caused a thin man prone on the ground with his Winchester pointing down the trackway to give a small cry of shock before he froze.

'You all right, Hank?'

There was no reply.

The robber's partner was spooked by the lack of reply. After many calls he became panicky and crossed the track and lumbered up the bank and into the thick undergrowth. He found Hank sitting with his back to a large tree and a look of terror on his face. Wide eyes and a tick-like repeated movement of his head indicated something to his left. Hank was wrong.

Jack Hoffmann's voice came out of nowhere. 'Got a good bead on you friend, with mah Winchester. Drop that pistol now, or you're a dead man.'

Jed dropped the Colt immediately. It slithered away down the bank.

'Now raise yourn hands and move next to Hank.'

The two stood by the big sycamore tree silently. There was no indication by direction or through any other means of where the deep, black molasses voice, which seemed bodiless, was coming from.

'Now, I think you have stolen some money from an old lady, a friend of mine. Got no proof on it. So you two varmints got but one choice. Dig out the money and return it to me. The alternative is I kill you here and now. Sorry ifn I got it wrong an' you're innocent fellas!' The silence was powerful. 'Be years afore they find your bones out here. Those are your horses tied over yonder pasture, I guess. Like I say, I got a good bead on you two and I'm keeping that bead until you take that money out of the saddlebags on each horse, place it in the burlap bag I can see on the cantle, put it on the ground, and git on yah ways. Any mischief and I'll blow yah both apart…'

Hoffmann watched from the undergrowth as the two would-be robbers walked back to their horses. Jed, without attempting to turn, his hands raised, offered to split the money three ways, but got no reply and after a long silence, did as he was bid. The two ruffians galloped off just as they had out of Longhorn town, as if the Devil was on their tail. Jack Hoffmann collected the burlap bag full of dollars and some jewellery, chuckling merrily to himself, and walked back to Jess.

Miss Pierce was astonished to see Mr Hoffmann again, and even more astonished to see her money: it was her life savings. Jack Hoffmann left without more ado, promising the town would be returned to normal soon.

NINE

The following day Micky Dobson had most everyone seated around his large country table at Double D ranch. 'OK,' said Micky. 'Let's get down to business. First of all congratulations to you all, particularly to you, Mr Hoffmann. Ezra McCormack's in jail, the rest of his evil gang are now dead and are to be buried soon by our mortician, Jethro Stone. 'Parently, their guns, horses and bit 'n pieces are to be auctioned and the dollars raised will go into the town's coffers.'

The rumble of voices and good words from mainly kin folks and close friends, who made up the top echelons of Longhorn's citizenry, was well received by Micky Dobson, who had been mightily relieved at the gang's demise.

'Mark Kidman's young brother,' he continued, 'has been dispatched to Harpersville where they now have a telegraph office. If you remember, Ian Duncan was dispatched to the sheriff at Harpersville a few weeks ago and was sadly murdered out on the range by one of the gang members. He was to have sent a telegraph message that Longhorn was being held to ransom by McCormack and his gang of cut-throats.

104

Now the way is clear for young Kevin to send a message I have worded asking for help from the law – in particular a circuit judge to send Ezra McCormack to the gallows – which with our town's collective skills could soon be erected!'

There was a great cheer to Micky's words. When the room fell to silence, he announced in rather formal tones, 'I believe Mr Hoffmann wants to say something.'

Jack leaned forward on the polished table, his dark eyes, jet black hair and handsome face, not to mention his large range-hardened build, suddenly dominated the gathering by its sheer presence. Nonetheless his words held them all by their sheer weight of argument and importance at that time in the early West.

'I kill bad men.' He looked around the gathering to gauge their reaction and got none. 'I also earn mah living by collecting bounty on these murderous villains, all of it law-abiding – including the killing I do. It's the law that is the keystone to this great country of ours.'

He looked about to see heads nodding and a few confirming words. 'But law ain't got out here in the places that I love. If there ain't no other way to stop 'em, I kill. Seems ta me that there ain't no option sometimes ta take such action as Jim and I have done yesterday. Killing folks is bad, but to let them continue their awful ways, in mah opinion, is worse.' Hoffmann took a slug of rye whiskey – Micky had discovered his favourite brand and had set a bottle and a glass in front of where he sat.

'Yuh needs to be mighty quick and strong to do what I do. I am lucky that men rarely want ta stand against me, and when they do I see fear in their eyes. I saw it in Coyote Kid before I killed him in a fair gunfight. Ifn you remember, those of yuh who saw the gunfight, I took his spurs and a silver chain from around his neck as some proof that I killed him, because there is a bounty out on him as a cold-blooded killer. If a few of you good folks who saw the fight could write out an affidavit that I took him in a fair fight, that would help me get the reward. As I say, I earn mah living by it.'

A number of voices rose, confirming that they would give him such an affidavit.

'That's the secret of law-abiding killing, people seeing that the other fella drew his gun first. It's the simple difference between staying free as honest men and murderous killers! And that's why I continue what I do for bounty and for the good of all. But it won't last forever. Ma prayers are that the law will get to these here parts soon, before I grow that mite bit slower and end up blown away in the dirt.'

Jack Hoffmann rarely smoked because he thought it could affect his speed, but he did at least accept that it was one of the ways in the West to relax; on this occasion he lifted a small gold case from his shirt pocket, took out a cheroot, struck a match on the heel of his boot and lit up the smoke. Jack could see the party were hanging on his every word, but he determined on not taking advantage of their stance. Yet he realized that this was opening the door to theirs and his own future. This was the town of his kin – people who were of his blood. Of his own choice Jack Hoffmann had always been a loner. But he knew, deep down, that he needed kin, like most of us. He knew that, and here was his one chance to help build the town – his town – a town he would adopt one day when his speed declined, and as he put it, became that mite slower. But until then...

'I want ta share something with yuh all. If it comes off, this town of Longhorn and me will benefit greatly. If it don't, then you folks at least will be none the worst for it. There is to be a gold shipment out to the railhead at Lusk in a few weeks' time on the Union Pacific railroad. I don't know 'zackly when, but I do know that a gang of evil hoodlums are planning to kill the posse – all of them – that has been set up to ride guard on a special wagon full of gold bars, then steal it when it's taken through Sharack County to the Lusk railhead. The county marshal has tipped me that this is about to happen because,' the gunfighter paused thoughtfully, 'I have gained a name back East 'bout mah methods that good folks think has some merit out here in the wilds, until the law is established.'

Jack took another slug of rye and stretched his long legs out under the large table to a whisper-fine silence. 'Normally I ride alone, but I have talked to Jim Bowry and he has agreed to ride with me to Sharack County.' A murmur of voices grew. 'Jim knows the score. Two of us against a large number of bad men who will kill for little reason, and gold, their deadly sin will fire them hugely. I am impressed by Jim Bowry. I believe we will be able to find a way to stop the gang – don't know how at this moment, the bounty reward will be huge and I think we will find a way. If we win, I intend to split it three ways – Jim, me and Longhorn town.'

There was sudden talk and raised voices of excitement. Micky Dobson called for silence because he could see that Jack Hoffmann wanted to continue.

'However, we have a problem. Jim's sister Nancy is a spunky gal by all accounts – she has even been known to break horses herself – but Nancy cannot be expected to run the place alone. She has folks there who work for Jim, but would any of yuh be willing to share the work and keep Jim and Nancy's horse-breaking enterprise going for a month or so whilst we are away?'

Micky Dobson stood up suddenly. 'You can count on us to help, Mr Hoffmann. Leave it with us, Jim, have an easy heart, my friend. Nancy knows us all. Just give us time to set this thing up. We won't let you down. When you come back all will be well, not to mention a few extra horses saddle-happy and ready for you to sell on!'

TEN

Jack Hoffmann reined his strong roan mare to a halt on the edge of a stubby hillock, and Cactus Jim Bowry pulled up his palomino gently beside him. Before them lay the Washakie Ridge – it dropped away before them in a ragged slope for 2,000 feet, with elm, oak, cedar and brushwood. The lower slopes beyond were interspersed with scrub grass and wildflowers: wild rose, rock penstemon, western red lily, and American holly. Much of nature's bounty could be admired as the slope fell away among rimrock and hill. Beyond lay the powerful glint of a distant river they needed to cross.

Both men had slept under the stars the previous night, the land about them giving up its senses and fragrances in the cooling night. They were intent on keeping away from the main trails – the secrecy of their journey into Sharack County, and finding out the location of Gene Pinder and his gang of ambitious gold robbers, was their first target. Surprise was the only strength they had at the moment, for at that point they did not have a concise plan of action. Much more was needed, and both gunfighters knew this was simply a scouting trip, a precursor to real action – speed was all.

Carefully the two range-hardened men rode their horses down the steep incline. Squawking crows flew about their nervous horses at first, as if telling the interlopers that their presence was unwelcome – then they were gone, and Washakie was theirs. They stopped at a spur of rock near the bottom, made a small fire and brewed up some coffee, which tasted good to dry throats. Over the hours they had ridden, their conversation fell to lives lived and battles fought in making the West what it was – Indians, Apaches, Comanches, Comancheros, the Civil War between the North and the Southern States – they considered how this land could now be the Confederate States of America if it hadn't been for Lincoln, great leaders on both sides and some luck. But never once did Jack Hoffman give away any clue of his own background, what had caused him to ride alone, taking the dangerous path to kill for money and bounty. His lips were sealed.

Cactus Jim grew to like Hoffmann, though; he respected him, anyone in the gunfighter's presence couldn't help but do that. Jim Bowry didn't pry into his new companion's closed world as they talked at length on their long ride – he was never even allowed into that inner world good friendship brings, yet mutual respect had grown between them, not born out of the skill in gun battle alone, but through something indefinable that one human being feels for another. They were by now, as the Indian Nations would call them, blood brothers – in all but the ceremonial mingling of their blood.

Both were attuned to their surroundings – every movement, every rustle of grass and foliage as they rode away from the bottom of the Washakie Ridge and into what had once been Indian land before the white men's big chiefs far away in Washington had sent them to reservations. After some hours they first heard Powder River before seeing it, and thirty minutes of riding at an easy pace saw them emerge among tall plants and ferns at the base of a large rock. There, thundering rapids ran to the right and left. They decided to go downstream instinctively, nothing said, Jack Hoffmann leading and the two rode on watching all around until they found a place that could be crossed. The river had widened considerably here and slowed to a dark meander. Nothing of any human habitation could be seen as far as either could make out.

Hoffmann loved the solitude. He felt safe here within the natural world. Mankind was his danger. Mountain lion, brown bear or rattler were dangers seen by many – but not to Jack Hoffman. Those crittas, as he would call them, were travellers on a path they shared – one giving way to the other when paths crossed, the crittas killing for food. They had never bothered him, and he didn't bother them. He felt an empathy for their animal spirits as his Indian friends has taught him, unlike other white men of his race.

Both horses, with encouragement, walked carefully into the water. Slowly the river rose about them until reaching their bodies. But no deeper did it climb. At length Jess and the palomino climbed out on to sweet and fertile green meadowland.

They found a place to camp after a short ride among some elm trees, cedar and quaking aspen. The latter made a fluttering sound from their leaves when hit by a breeze. This eerie sensation was nothing at all to the range riders. Indeed they found it soothing as they lit their camp fire and set up camp. After a hearty meal of sausages, heated beef jerky, potatoes and cabbage, which Jim had added to his gunny sack before they left, the two sat by the fire as the night-time stars appeared, light blue turned to darkness revealing more stars; they talked on, making plans.

'I knows the land around here quite well,' offered Jim. 'My pa used to do trade with the Indians – vittles and medicine mainly, they had secrets 'bout plants that only the red men knows – one tribe to another, passing it on.' Jim built himself a quirly and lit it with a burning stick from the fire. 'Figure we need to talk some, 'bout our next move, Jack.'

Jack Hoffmann's respect for his companion grew more as their conversation continued and as Bowry revealed his backwoodsman past. As a young boy he had sometimes even accompanied his father into Indian sacred lands before they had been removed to a reservation. It was now only a mile away. The Spanish called that type of region a mesa, or table-land. The Indians lived all about happily, but believed this raised land to be sacred, only to be entered by men of good heart. 'They must have thought my pa a good 'n, to let him and me go up there, I guess.'

He pulled on his quirly and told the story of that wild and wooded high ground ahead of them, and how the small Indian nation had been moved out in great, sad columns; buffalo skin tepees or sick beds pulled by ponies, women, children and warriors walking away from a land that had been their forefathers for many centuries before the white man had arrived. He cut a small branch from a willow tree and whittled it with his Bowie knife to turn the white wood into a small flute, which he played a merry tune on, then used it to make the call of wild birds. Jack's dark eyes and sombre face never gave away how impressed he was by this skill.

The backwoodsman part of Cactus Jim Bowry fell to reminiscing on times past, as the sun dipped below the trees and the fire blazed up with new kindling, telling of the now empty Indian sacred land, of how good it was to be there, and how his father had continued to roam all over the mesa for many things that could be eaten or sold in town, which the Indians had shown him before they had been moved away. This high ground Jim also believed was magic in some way, because the Indians had told his father so. And they had been there for centuries, so who was to argue with that? It was a good place to live in and be.

Full of unexpected passion, Jim continued telling the bounty hunter about government surveyors who had been sent out west to reconnoitre the area in the 1790s around eighty years before. The mesa was only about a mile ahead from where they had set up camp. It rose a thousand feet, and spread for only about ten miles at most in any direction. Few people knew of its existence. Two narrow rising areas of ground allowed the top of the mesa to be reached by horse or on foot; the remaining sides were cliffs or steep slopes at best. Jim determined that the gold-carrying wagon and team of six horses would travel across at the far end where there was a good navigable road leading from Fort Carmin to Lusk. It ran from west to east on the lower ground they were part of. Jim suggested they needed to take one side of the mesa or the other with care, to search out Gene Pinder and his riders.

Jack Hoffmann suggested they split up to ride each side of the mesa to its far end, then share their knowledge. Jim nodded his agreement. There was a small river that ran down at the end – it couldn't be missed as there was a waterfall at the bottom which could be heard from some distance. They agreed on meeting there, where the water joined the lower ground at a waterfall.

***

Jack Hoffmann arrived at the waterfall early the next day. He could hear the sound of tumbling water, and walked Jess into a wonderful, peaceful bower, such was the confined beauty of the place his guard dropped briefly, but he quickly returned his legendary sharpness. He had been looking upwards as he followed the sounds of water flow, and could see a little river working its way down from the Indians' sacred ground a thousand feet above. Something like thirty feet above him, the river fell over a rock lip and dropped into a silvered pool where fishes swam. Willow, cottonwood and osiers dug their roots into the sweet, wet soil around a deep pool.

He took Jess over to the pool where she drank her fill; he broke open a pack from the two gunny sacks tied to the saddle and took out cooking utensils. Soon a pan was steaming over the fire, and he added some Arbuckle to the boiling water, then tipped eggs and bacon into a frying pan. Breakfast, washed down with lashings of steaming hot coffee, set him up for the day and all that must be ahead. It was a good meal, the best he had enjoyed for a long while. The solitary openness of the wild was the best companion the bounty hunter knew, and the only close one he needed right then.

It didn't take long for Jim Bowry to find him, thanks to the backwoodsman that lurked inside the tough range-hardened individual. Hoffmann did not hear or see a thing as he downed the last of his coffee – but suddenly he turned abruptly, the Colt brought to killing position in that same moment.

'Was gonna tap you on the shoulder, Jack, but you were too quick for me!' The cheerful, bronzed face of Cactus Jim Bowry appeared by a stand of cottonwoods. 'Any coffee left?' He crossed the distance in a few steps and bent down by the campfire.

'Made enough for two. Where you been?'

'I was up 'afore dawn. Scouting, as you might say, and found out some interesting news. I've had no breakfast and I'm starving hungry.'

The big man got up nimbly. 'Cook you something. Whilst I do, tell me your news.'

Bowry sat by the fire, the early chill of the night still in him, and he explained all that he had found. It seemed that not far from where they were camping, one of the two narrow slopes where they could access the full way up to the top of the mesa was only a short distance away. Jim would have scouted it, but in the half-darkness it was too dangerous. He said no more until he got his meal of eggs, bacon, beans and coffee.

'Thanks, Jack.' He continued between much appreciated bites and told of his roughly laid out plan. To the right of the little river high above them was a cliff, a vertical drop that gave an uninterrupted view of the road almost directly below. One could see a good mile in the direction of Fort Carmin, so anyone up there on the clifftop would get good warning of the gold wagon's approach.

Jim finished, put his plate down on the fine green sward, and started on his mug of coffee. 'The road runs directly below the cliff. I have travelled this part of the road when Pa was alive for business for him – crafty old fella he was, too – so's I knows that the only place to make a grab at that gold wagon – militia guard an' all – would be right under this cliff.' He took a long drink at his coffee and wiped his lips.

116

'Why? 'Cos there's rocks all around. Some have been moved to the side of the road by the road builders, some were too big to move – but all of them gives a wonderful cover for an ambush.' He looked across to Jack Hoffman, who was staring into nothing, deep in thought.

'From up there, you say about a thousand feet, a Winchester would be hard pressed to take a man out, at, say, four hundred yards. Could be done, but we need more certainty.' He paused, looking back at the stilled face. 'But a long-barrelled Sharps would do it!'

The bright, range-hardened expression returned. 'Yeah. You're right Jack. Sharps is the best long-range rifle yer can get. A thousand yards, no bother, and a sure killing range of five hundred to a rifleman with good eyesight. Mine's perfect. How about you?'

The bounty hunter just nodded silently. 'Single shot, though. Big 'uns got a bore of half an inch. Some kick on it. You couldn't fire from the hip, casual like. Got to settle down on the ground with a dolly-stick support.'

'No problem. Takes our time. Sets oursel' up, easy like.'

Hoffmann stared at Jim Bowry, weighing things. 'Single shot, though..'

'I know. It's a specialist weapon. They reckon a good man can get through about eight cartridges a minute, and there's two of us.'

'Cartridges instead o' shells?'

'They're made up specially. Black powder. You can even get yer own mix on it.' Jim Bowry grinned. Jack could see that it looked as if his range partner was taking to the whole thing now.

'OK, Jim. Let's go up top of this here mesa and take a look at your shootin' gallery.'

ELEVEN

Kate Strong was stood behind the bar of the Midnight Star as usual when a youngster came through the batwing doors. Her green eyes latched on to him out of curiosity at first, before she recognized him.

'Buddy Cooper! What you doing here in Hardins Bluff?'

His boyish face looked a little abashed. 'Want to see Mr Hoffmann, ma'am, if'n I may?'

'He's not here, Buddy. Why do you want to see him?'

'Ma done told me that I gotta get work or we're in trouble. Tried all around these here parts, but folks say I'm a gunsel after I stood up to Abe Kilroy, and that I would bring trouble with me. Can't get no work anywhere, and I need to see Mr Hoffmann urgent.'

At that moment Thomas the barkeep lifted the flap of the counter and joined her.

'Would you get Sammy to collect the glasses and taken them out for washing?'

She turned back to the gangly youth, thought for a moment, then said: 'Buddy, I want your word on what I'm about to tell you.'

119

'Yes, Ma'am,' he answered quickly.

Kate indicated to him to follow, and took him through to a back room next to her parlour. 'You heard of them new telegraph offices where folks can send messages from town to town over hundreds of miles?'

Buddy nodded. 'Yes, ma'am.'

'Well, I have been given a telegraph message about a hold-up. I can't tell you more, Buddy, but Mr Hoffmann is now on his way to Longhorn, then on to help out because there is a bounty involved.'

'You think I should follow him?'

'Not normally. But you do seem in some trouble. You don't want to let your ma down, and I think Jack might write you a note perhaps, that you could show folks saying that you were good and trustworthy and you have given up gunfighting for good.'

'But I have, Ma'am, you knows that.'

'Other folks don't, Buddy. A note from Mr Hoffmann might do the trick.'

With profuse thanks Buddy Cooper left the Midnight Star and rode down the long backwoods trail to Longhorn town. Soon he had left the tough countryside holding beeves and sheep where he had been born and self-raised. Here lay great rolling grasslands and fertile steppes with handsome rivers flowing through them. Buddy rode on with speed. His palomino gelding was a strong, easy horse, good tempered and brave. The trail began winding down from dark woodlands in the north and slipped away over a broad meadow towards the beckoning south lands where he was heading. As he rode on determinedly, the geographical features now turned to an immense sweep of rocky terrain, rising steeply from the floor of a verdant valley, to form a massive wall crowning the uplands section of a great ranch.

His route along the trail ran along the foot of the highlands, and soon he could see a turf house and a shack just off the trail. The sun was dropping low across the sky, and he wondered if the owner would give him shelter for the night. As Buddy arrived it was nearing dusk and when he knocked at the rickety door of the shack a man in his forties opened it immediately as if he had seen the stranger riding up. The man held a Tranter rifle in his left hand, butt on the floor, but the implication was obvious.

'Wadya want?'

Buddy touched the brim of his Stetson. 'Sorry 'bout bothering you, sir, but I wonder if you could give me some shelter for the night?'

His wife looked over the man's shoulder. 'We've had ranger-riders here 'afore, an' they always was a problem in some ways or other.'

The sharecropper looked Buddy up and down. 'What's those pistols doing on yourn hips?' Before Buddy could reply he continued. 'This here is our land, signed for under President Lincoln's bill, which gives anyone the right to settle unoccupied land out West. We've had trouble with a bully who wants to throw us off.'

Buddy thought of the large ranch he had seen high up behind the shack.

'But I also knows the unwritten law of the West 'bout giving shelter and food to a stranger. Trouble is, we don't know who the hell you are.' He paused, then said, 'There's a turf house out back where we started out, made a few dollars and then built this here shack. Our animals now live there. If needs drive yer, you can bed down there and my wife will bring yer some vittles'

Buddy was touched by the offer, considering how they must be in fear of their situation, if not their lives. He thanked them and led his horse into the humble dwelling. He was tired, and ate the gruel the woman brought out, then settled down for a sleep that promised to refresh his tired body and mind. But he was woken just after dawn by the sound of someone forcing their way into the share-croppers' shack.

Buddy Cooper was up in a moment. He put on his gun-rig quickly, went outside and ran across to the shack, pushing himself hard against the clapboard wall. The talking was quite plain to hear and the message plain to understand through the wall. The ranch owner wanted these two-range scum, as he named them, off his land so he could spread his ownership further. Yes, they were sharecroppers, and yes, they had put their mark on so-called legal documents, but President Lincoln was now dead and buried. Mr Smith had made an offer, which they were very stupid not to take up, and to give them some incentive they would break the place up a little first.

But before they could make a start Buddy Cooper came through the rickety door, not quite knowing what he would say. He didn't need to worry. One of the men, dressed in quality buckskins and holding a Winchester, turned towards the intruder with it coming up towards killing position. Buddy Cooper's draw was like lightning, and the boom of the Peacemaker shattered the strained silence of the room and drove the rifle from the man's hands.

'My ma says you shouldn't talk to folks like that. 'Part from being illegal wanting to throw this man and his wife off their land, it's just plain wrong. They's sharecroppers.' The silence hung in the stillness for a while until the smoke cleared. The man with the rifle spoke.

'Who are you? And what are you doing out here? Does your ma know you're out?' He smirked at his comrade.

Three clicks from Buddy's six-gun as he pulled the hammer back pulled the man up almost to attention. It also did something else, which the self-conscious gunfighter felt was a lie that must be said. 'My ma said that I must look after my uncle and aunt – make sure they're all right. My Pa heads up the Cooper gang, an' if folks wants to push them around to let him know.'

'Never heard of your pa.'

'I'll ask him to drop into that big ranch house up yonder on the ridge.' Buddy smiled for the first time for effect. He didn't like lying one bit, but felt it had to be done. 'I'm leaving this morn and will be sure to give them all your regards.' He smiled again, that special smile that Fate had now given him. 'Either way, gentlemen, he'll be sure to keep an eye out for his brother and his wife.'

The two bullyboys left with angry looks on their faces.

The sharecropper stood shaking his head as they mounted their horses and galloped away. His wife said, 'Well, young man, that takes the biscuit. You wants some breakfast, I think you've earned it.'

The dangerous title of Kid Cooper, which he now felt sure rested on his shoulders after this crazy episode, was not an easy title of so-called Western honour to take on – at least for him. Buddy rode away after that huge breakfast and was soon back on the trail that led towards Longhorn. All he wanted was a job to help out his ma, and Mr Hoffmann to give him a letter of introduction, saying he had given up gunfighting for good. And now this.

TWELVE

Once led out of the bower, their horses ready and alert, Jack Hoffmann and Jim Bowry mounted up, moving on to open range below the mesa, the man-made road directly ahead. Nothing was in sight. Side by side they rode easily along the beaten down dirt roadway until Jim indicated for them to turn off into shrub and mesquite. Unless one knew, the rising slope was hidden from view from the road completely. Behind them lay great wild grasslands and distant fertile steppes, certainly with handsome rivers flowing through them. They rode in carefully through a narrow opening, where soon after, thick clumps of walnut, oak, elderberry and buttonwood abounded. Jim pointed out the land either side of the rise, which was rich with edible game: quail, wild chicken and turkey. No wonder the Indian tribe had flourished here for centuries before they were forced on to a reservation.

The dimming light of the woods fell away as they rose towards higher ground…birds twittered, a leaf fell from a tree as they climbed in near silence, the small sounds serving to emphasize that silence. Hoffmann was in an area he didn't know, and realized he was holding his breath for long moments even though there was no obvious reason for doing so. Was it too quiet maybe?

'Do you feel it?'

Jack Hoffman looked at his partner but didn't answer.

'The Indians said this is a special place. Pa told me so. Magic, he said. Don't know 'bout such things. Pa and me, when I was a kid and the Indians were here, said we could take some vittles and sleeping stuff up here 'cos they liked Pa and said it would make us strong. T'was amazing that they would let whites do that. I asked him you know, he said they called it their sacred ground, but it were something else too. It were a special place fer goodness an' to help good people. They buried their dead up there in wrappings above the ground among the trees. If we went there we would be killed – even me as a boy.' He took a swig from a water bottle and turned to the silent rider at his side. 'So, like me, you can feel something powerful up here?'

Jack Hoffmann had seen many things, ridden many places, both wild and far from civilization, and in among struggling townships across the West. Always he kept his own council. A solitary loner who rarely spoke of his thoughts to others. Cactus Jim Bowry had got as near as another human being could get to the inner man. 'Yeah. I feels something, Jim. Mebbe it is special here. Don't hold with…' He broke off, then added, 'Guess when you're dead, you're dead…'

They climbed further in silence, and Jim said, 'Like you, I don't hold with mumbo jumbo either. The Indians knew so much that we so-called civilized peoples don't know. Pa said that.'

'What happened to him?'

Jim was quiet for some moments, and then he said at a run, 'A rattler got him when he was making camp. I was thirteen then, out collecting wood for the fire. I helped him up on to his horse and we got back to Aunt Louise's turf house, where he died. Ma had passed on the year before, so's I was on my own at thirteen. Worked at living, though. Uncle Thomas, Pa's elder brother, took me in, and here I am now.' Jim Bowry took another swig from his water bottle. 'You, Jack? No point in asking 'bout you, I 'spose?'

The gunfighter rode on silently for some time, then answered: 'No point.'

They reached the top in five more minutes, and Jim led the way through strong, verdent greenwood, and soon came to the cliff top. The ground beneath their feet was nearly solid rock, and the area ahead to the cliff was therefore almost totally free of plants and grass. As they walked across it, the special feeling they had felt within the luxuriant wood and forest vanished. Neither spoke of it.

'Well, wasn't I right, Jack? 'Bout the view down?'

The tall, dark man looked down a thousand feet, his eyes surveying the scene carefully. 'Yes, you were, Jim. This and a good Sharps rifle is perfect.' Beneath them, the dirt road was merely a faint line. But either side of it, directly beneath the cliff, were many boulders.

'We could set ourselves up, the Sharps barrels resting on dolly-stick supports, and we'd be able to take out them bad men one at a time as clear as you like.' He turned. 'Trouble is, we don't know where and when.'

Jim was looking towards forested land rising up from the gulley on the side of the mesa along which Hoffman had ridden to meet up at the waterfall. A man was riding an appaloosa horse into the forest. Jim quickly took out a spy-scope from his saddlebag and targeted the rider. 'He's got a rifle in his saddlebag and two handguns on his hips.'

'Could be some fella making his way to find Gene Pinder's hideout at that old mine.''My thoughts exactly. Let's follow him.'

'Time we get down there he could be a long ways ahead.'

Jim Bowry grinned. 'We can follow his trail, no problem.'

Together they were up in leather and riding down the grass incline.

***

Joshua Petersen was riding easy. He had waited a good month before travelling down to see Gene Pinder and his gang, because he knew that his old buddy-in-arms, Tom Wolff, would be there by now and could give him some back-up for joining the gang. His half-brother, Mordecai, had filled him in with more details, including the likely date – within a few days, he couldn't be sure of it for certain – for the gold wagon to be taken from Fort Carmin to the Lusk railhead. All was in the waiting now. The gang posted a lookout every day from dawn to dusk.

As Joshua rode his big appaloosa stallion along the trail, he could see the lookout through the trees. Joshua's old buddy in crime, Tom Wolff, would know about farmer Moses' death, he was sure, because he knew of the farmer through his family's wholesale business, buying green stuff. Already the word of the gunfight outside the Midnight Star would have travelled far. Jacob Moses was a very fast new gunsel who had proved it to the whole of Goodland county, and someone had killed him. But who? Joshua Petersen was about to announce his new status.

He could see the derelict mine now. The large wooden buildings were still in a reasonable state, but inside there was much decay. The Page Mining Corporation had been struggling to keep going, not because the open-cast coal mine was short of coal – in fact they were at the point of sinking a new shaft to get at the reserves below ground – but because Morgan Reeves had robbed a stagecoach stopping there with dollars on board for the miners' pay. After that and the riot that followed, the firm went under.

Petersen tied his horse to the hitching rail outside the main entrance, and, fully tooled up, strode through the doors of the main office. There were six men inside, including Gene Pinder, who stepped out from the group. 'Who are you and what do ya want here?' His eyes fell on the two Colts on the stranger's hips.

'Looking fer work. Got anything going?'

Six men stared at the one standing there – but he was a helluva guy. There was something menacing about him, even though he was outgunned six to one. The full Mexican-style moustache seemed to highlight the hard planes of his evil face. Not the sort of fella you'd be happy to mess with.

But Gene Pinder had the talent to be head of this gang of toughs. He was no fool. He could kill, he had killed before, and he knew how to survive such skirmishes. The nastier they were, the better for this heist, he knew – providing he kept everyone cowed by his own six-gun, his speed with it, and the belief that each man's part of the robbery would make them rich beyond their dreams.

'What sort of work can you offer?'

'Robbery.' Joshua Petersen was full of confidence, and needed it.

The silence was total.

'I killed Jacob Moses in a fair gunfight. Him against me. I wuz quicker. There's a man here I worked with on a heist. Tom Wolff and I done a heist down Wichita way, years ago. We wuz never caught, 'cos we're both professionals.' Two diamond-sharp blue eyes stared across the six without a flicker. 'You wanta give me backing, Tom?'

A harsh, guttural voice spoke out from the group. 'Yeah. I knows this guy. Worked with him. Don't know 'bout this here gunfighting rep he's claiming against Jacob Moses, though. Sure, Moses killed Mal Quincy in a fair fight in Hardins Bluff and that got him a powerful rep. No one knows who killed Jacob Moses, but I do know that some son-of-a-bitch shot him clean through the head...'

Petersen folded his arms across his tasselled deer-hide jacket. 'It was me. Any of you fellas what to step outside and find out how fast I am?'

Gene Pinder stepped forward, raised his hands wide and turned around. 'OK. That's enough. I'm leader here. No one's outgunning anyone, you can be sure on it. We're here to do a job.' His powerful slit eyes fell on Petersen, and he walked up to him, his staring brown eyes inches from Petersen's face. 'Kill me ifn you can, buddy, and five good men behind me will blow you to bits.'

He swung around, then back to the stranger. 'But if you can add to this professional heist of millions, always under my command, you're in, Petersen. Whad'yer say?'

The two men held their stare, eyeball to eyeball, neither giving an inch. Suddenly Joshua Petersen stepped back. 'Aye, boss. Yes, I'd like ta join ya, Mr Pinder.'

***

Carefully Jack and Cactus Jim Bowry moved silently away from the windowless side of the mine, and walked back to their horses tethered seventy yards away in the wood. They climbed back into leather and rode back towards the mesa.

'You heard the date for the wagon leaving Fort Carmin?'

'Yeah. Fifteenth of July. That's a month's time. We've enough time to get back to Longhorn, buy those Sharps rifles and set things up. But we don't want ta do this without some back-up. We'll go see Micky Dobson and get the committee's OK afore coming back with them their Sharps. What do you say, Jack?'

Hoffmann was riding quietly, deep in thought. 'Yeah. We'll do just that..' He looked across, dark eyes glowering beneath the black, low-crown Stetson, 'I knew that date in mah head 'afore the guy said it.'

They rode on for a few minutes, carefully weaving among the undergrowth when Jim replied. 'Strange… so did I. What the hell is happening? Don't believe in no Indian mumbo jumbo though… Anyways we've both heard it said in that there mine building.'

THIRTEEN

Nine men were settled excitedly around Micky Dobson's large, polished country table with drinks and smoking. Micky was at the head, Jack Hoffmann at the other end, and the remaining seven were sitting three one side as before, and four at the other, including Cactus Jim, the horse breaker.

'Before you start telling us what you and Jim Bowry have found out – and I know it's about this here bounty money you are after – I've got someone outside who knows ya. I don't know if ya want to know him, though.' Micky Dobson looked around the gathering, wise eyes on someone who had surprisingly seen only twenty-three summers. 'The boy's name is Buddy Cooper, known also as Kid Cooper. 'Apparently with your help, he has got on his feet now and aims to find a job.' Dobson looked very serious. 'I think he wants to work with you, get advice, but he won't say. Frankly he seems pretty naive to me.'

Jack Hoffmann didn't shown the smallest amount of the surprise that he actually felt.

'I can take you out to the trophy room where he is – or I can get one of my boys to send him on his way with a six-gun in his back. Choice is yours, Mr Hoffmann.'

The big man rose easily. 'Be obliged to meet him, Mr Dobson.'

Buddy Cooper was admiring the trophies around the walls when Jack walked in. Dobson pulled the door shut behind them.

'I hope you don't mind me askin' after you, Mr Hoffmann. But Ma done thinks I should be doing a sight more than practisin'. Wants me to get some money coming in. I done rebuilt the pigsty, done a lot of fencing work all the way down to the brook, and stopped the leak in the roof of the house. But Ma says we need money soon or we're in trouble. So's I've come to see you, Mr Hoffmann. Miss Strong says you might write me a letter to say I'm OK and trustworthy. That business with Abe Kilroy is putting folks off employing me. They say I'm troublesome. '

Before Jack Hoffmann stood a tall youth, no more than twenty years old, whom he knew well: still with a freckled baby face, the bright blue eyes had an innocence built into his psyche somehow. Even though he had only deliberately winged the other man in the gunfight, the word was out now that Buddy Cooper was a killer. It might have been his upturned nose that was the last piece to the jigsaw puzzle that made Buddy Cooper look much more of a boy than really he was, and this must have given would-be gunfighters the thought that this boy was for the taking. Now he stood before one of the West's greatest gunfighter with an apparent innocence that would have taken most people's breath away. The gangly lad was dressed in a fancy embroidered calico shirt, brown pants, hand-tooled short riding boots, and a near-white Stetson in his hand. Tied down on his thighs were two immaculate Colt Peacemakers.

'You brought proper range gear with you?'

The boy nodded. 'Yes, sir.'

'Your mother know that already you've fought men with a six-gun?'

'My ma is one tough lady, Mr Hoffmann. She couldn't have survived out in Water Creek if she hadn't been.' Buddy shuffled his feet. 'Ma don't ask no questions, and I don't say.'

Hoffmann nodded. 'You been practising with your guns?'

'Yeah. Can hit a dime stood on edge at thirty yards with my Winchester rifle.'

'You ever fired a Sharps long-barrelled carbine?'

'No, sir. Why do you ask?'

Hoffmann waved the remark aside.

'Would you be willing to kill men, bad men, in cold blood?'

'No, sir. I don't think I rightly could.'

'To save someone's life?'

'Maybe. Don't know until I'm there, sir.'

The bounty hunter walked across the room slowly and looked out of the window. Without turning he said, 'I've known yah for some time, Buddy. Mah judgement is that if I tells yah something and that it must not go any further, you would stick by that.'

The young freckled face looked serious, and he nodded. 'Yes, sir.'

Hoffmann turned. 'There's a shipment of gold bars being taken from Fort Carmin to the railhead in Lusk. In just over a week a gang of hoodlums plans to hold up the heavy wagon taking the gold bars. My partner and I aim to hold them to a Mexican stand-off from a high cliff with Sharps long-range rifles. If we can stop the heist, the bounty reward will be huge. I plan to give some of it to this here town over yonder, Longhorn, for reasons of my own. You ken?'

'I understand, sir. Will you cut me in, and what pay would I get?'

Jack Hoffmann smiled. The boy had learned some. 'Part of the bounty reward,' he said with a smile, 'but I don't know what it'll be. You can trust me, Buddy Cooper. It will be a fair distribution. You mustn't tell anyone, though. Not even your ma. What do you think she would say, if she knew?'

Kid Cooper looked around the room. 'Don't give that sort of thing a lotta time. Like I say, she's one tough lady. Guess she'd say I'm a grown man now and must make my own ways in this world. She always says, treat people right, and mostly they will do the same for you. But bad men are bad men, and I'm learning quick about them, Mr Hoffmann, so's I kin survive.'

A minute later they returned to Micky Dobson's grand parlour. The gunfighter brought in Buddy Cooper, and they stood before the eight gathered at the huge table.

'Don't worry about the dude clothing. This here is a friend of mine. I will vouch for him in spite of his apparent naïve appearance. He's brought the usual range gear with him, and will change his cloths immediate.' He looked at Buddy as if it were a command.

'Pull a chair up for the young man, would you, Ernest? Put it next to Mr Hoffmann's chair,' said Micky Dobson amiably. 'Now, Jack – may I call you Jack?'

'Please do,' the reply from the deep voice slipped smoothly across the table like black molasses.

'You've been outa town some time, and we're all keen to know where you and Jim Bowry have been, and how, if anything, this scouting trip will help us here with the troubles the McCormack gang have caused us? What can you tell us?'

Cactus Jim, always ready to engage in any matter whether it was a fight or straightforward talking, leaned on the table among the others. 'We need two,' he looked at Buddy Cooper, 'mebbe three Sharps rifles by tomorrow!'

Jack Hoffmann told of the heist, their plan for a Mexican stand-off from the high cliff at the mesa. How they proposed to stop the bad men, and to allow the shipment to travel on safely to the railhead at Lusk.

'So, as Jim says, we need three Sharps rifles and a lot of ammo by tomorrow so we can return and be set up ready before the shipment begins its travel. There will be a great bounty given for stopping this gold heist, which is owned by the federal government. I give my word here and now that the bounty will be split fairly, so that we three gunsels will get a fair share of it for our work, and the rest will go into Longhorn town's bank under the watchful eyes of the Longhorn town's committee, to be used to repair the damage caused by the McCormack gang. The remainder can be used to help this town prosper.'

'You think there's that much coming from such a bounty, Jack?'

'A quarter of a million dollars in gold? What do you think, Mr Dobson?'

A great deal of excitement filled the room. Micky Dobson, chairman of the committee, shouted for silence and got it. 'Right. Listen up, you all. I propose that we find the money for these here three carbines.'

'And the ammo,' added Jim Bowry.

'And the ammo, too. We, the committee, will own these carbines, and whilst our erstwhile posse, for want of a word, is away on our behalf, we ask Luke Schwab – our town's solicitor, lawyer and bookkeeper all joined into one, 'cos there's no one else so qualified around these here parts – to draw up a bill of words that will make us all legit. That all right with you, Luke?'

The dapper man smiled, adjusted his bow tie. 'Of course, Micky.'

The chairman looked around the table. 'Do we have agreement, then?'

There was huge agreement to this, and Ernest Kane suggested that his brother, Peter, should take the money and buy the guns, as he knew a lot about the Sharps weapon from work as a bison hunter when he was young. Micky Dobson said, as head of the committee, he would accompany Peter that afternoon. Everyone agreed to this.

Micky Dobson took money from his safe somewhere in the huge ranch house – no one except Micky knew exactly where it was – and the two men set off for Longhorn in his buggy.

With the demise of the McCormack gang, folks were out on the streets all over town making repairs, replacing broken windows, painting and the like. Old Matthew Stoner called out to Micky as the wagon passed the livery stable saying that Ezra McCormack was safely locked up in his own jail house awaiting Sheriff Clark's arrival soon from Harpersville. They stopped the buggy and continued talking for a while, Matthew Stoner explaining how Cactus Jim's bullet only went through McCormack's hand and did no other damage to it. He kicked up one hell of a row, though, saying he was an innocent man who was attacked for no reason, and he was going to tell the sheriff all about it. The agreement was that this was the best thing to happen.

Ten minutes later they pulled up outside Tex Ware and Son's gunshop. Micky Dobson led the way in, a bell on the door tinkling to call for service. The head of the new town's committee had been thinking, as they drove in, that it was OK to let Tex know about the forming of the committee, now that the gang had been vanquished, but not about his reason for the requirement of three Sharps carbines. He and

Peter Kane had talked this over on the way into town and decided that secrecy was the best policy for the moment. All would be revealed later if the posse of three won their battle.

The shop was well stocked with gun racks all around the walls, and the window was also full of many guns. Tex Ware came up from out the back. He had long, bushy grey sideburns and wore thin-framed spectacles on a large hooked nose. 'Hello – Micky Dobson and Peter Kane isn't it? What can I do for you gentlemen?' He leaned on the long wooden counter, a smile on his worldly face and oil stains on his hands from repair work.

Micky smiled in return, a look of seriousness on his strong, brown face. 'As you may have heard, we set up a citizens' committee immediately after the McCormack boys came into town, where we hoped to keep things in check. It didn't work out too well, I must admit – at least until the gunfighter Jack Hoffmann came to town.'

'The fella who shot the Coyote Kid?'

'The very same. He works under our orders. Clearly it had to be a secret then, because if the gang had found out, every man jack of us could have been in real trouble. Anyways, with their destruction I, as the chairman, will be happy for the rest of the town to know about us now. There is more to tell – but not yet. We can't say yet. Only that we need to purchase from you three Sharps long-range rifles. Do you stock them, Tex?'

'Yes, sir,' beamed the Texan shop keeper with a big smile of pleasure. 'Got to say, though, that these here weapons will throw a slug over a thousand yards without any difficulty and will kill for sure at five hundred, but you need sharp eyes to do it, 'cos five hundred yards is a hell of a distance. But because of this long-range ability the Sharps carbines cost more than yer average rifle.'

Peter Kane nodded acknowledgement for what the shop keeper was saying. 'Yeah, I knows this, Tex. Did a bit of buffalo shooting with one when I was in my younger years. Can we have a look at one?'

Tex soon returned with the special rifle from out the back, and handed it over to Peter. It was a large gun, fully four feet long. With the butt resting on the ground, the end of the barrel came up to Peter's chin. He hefted it, opened the single-shot breach and inspected the bore for any scoring, and asked: 'This new?'

'Yes, sir. Got three available for you gentlemen. Brand new. For the Longhorn committee's use. No questions asked. Got a stack of cartridges for the Sharps carbine, too.'

They discussed the black powder mix, the size of the bullet and the sighting arrangement in detail while Micky Dobson listened intently. He respected the other two men's knowledge and experience, realizing that these guns, and all guns in general, were deadly killing machines. He didn't give much thought to it normally, too busy running Double D.

141

All men needed them out here in the Wild West, where dangerous crittas abounded, and honest folks needed protecting from those and from bad men alike. Micky, like folks all over Wyoming and beyond, knew that a gun was a tool for survival. He normally gave little thought to the future, too busy with the dangerous present, but there in that gun shop, as Micky Dobson listened, he wondered if this great country, with so many advances being made, would still be hefting guns after the law arrived.

They carefully loaded up the wagon with their precious cargo, wrapped up well by Tex and his son so prying eyes were not encouraged to look. At one o'clock they were back at the Double D ranch and settled with the others for the midday meal of large steaks, grits and vegetables from their gardens. Afterwards they met outside where a long piece of open land climbed away to nothing. The place was clear of beeves, sheep and anything that could fall foul of their shooting. They set up a line of empty bottles at one hundred yards and loaded the Sharps rifle under the guidance of Jack Hoffmann and Peter Kane. Everyone on the committee, including the solicitor Luke Schwab, wanted to take a shot. Buddy, the youngest, was chosen to try first.

He lay down, set up the carbine on the dolly-stick rest, and took a careful aim at the central bottle. He could hardly see it, but found that by focusing his eye and attuning his mind to the faint target, just as he did when practising back home at Water Creek, he could take a good, steady aim. Slowly squeezing the trigger brought a huge detonation, and the great kick at his shoulder lifted him somewhat. Buddy reasoned that he hadn't been ready for this force, and would allow for the shock in future.

Micky Dobson looked through his field glasses and proudly announced the bottle was no longer there. He thought he could see its pieces far beyond the row. A cheer went up. Everyone still wanted to try out the gun, but Dobson said that only those who were going to be using these long-range rifles – just the three men, Fred Kidman, who had some experience of the Sharps, Cactus Jim Bowry, and the new young-ster, Buddy Cooper – could now show what they could do. He added that this test was only at one hundred yards, and the killing range of the Sharps – if it came to killing – was at five hundred yards from the top of a cliff. Everyone hoped that the idea of a Mexican stand-off would succeed, but if it didn't, they were well armed, and well placed to kill as many bad men as needs took. It was this advantage that gave them hope of success.

Jack Hoffman had weighed up the plan in his mind over the weeks of planning, and decided to explain that he had made an alteration to it, before anyone got further excited. That deep, black molasses voice cut through the bonhomie. He told them that he had recruited Fred Kidman, who had arrived that morn-ing from town, to take his place because of his expe-rience. He had decided that the three riflemen up on the mesa cliff top would need back-up that could come closer to the action. Yes, he acknowledged the high cliff vantage point, and that the Sharps long-range carbines were the best answer to the Pinder gang's attempt to steal the gold bullion wagon. But it needed more. He intended to lead three men, all good shots with Winchesters, to shoot up the gang from a small wood that gave a wide view of the rock-filled terrain where the heist was due to occur. Everyone was suddenly taken by surprise.

'Cactus Jim knows these men, enough to say they're reliable men. They're all good fellas and kin folks to you all in some ways or other.'

Hoffmann put his hands on his hips, dark eyes swung around the gathering. 'Done talked this idea of mine over with your chairman and Cactus Jim. Got their approval immediate. Jim told me about three likely men and where I could find them: Colin Harris, Bill Waterford and Tommy Dobson. I rode back into town, and they'll be over in a couple of days, ready to work with me from that wood. With the end of McCormack, town's all a-go with repairs, so's a vacation has been declared to allow the work to get done. Seems everyone's holding fire on business doings until the work is finished. Goodwill Western style is all over Longhorn now, and folks have said they'll do the work that Colin, Bill and Tommy needed to attend, whilst they are away.'

FOURTEEN

Morgan Philips had recently accepted the offer to head up the civilian militia by the commander of Fort Carmin. The fort so far out in Wyoming was thought to be fairly safe from robbery at this major level, and as costs had become an issue, the commander wanted to address other changes as well, hoping that a good report might get him back nearer civilization. It also saved state troopers for other, more specific duties that could only be carried out by enlisted men. Although Philips had been an officer in the US Cavalry, he needed to recruit six civilian men from the area to accompany the gold bullion wagon, three either side of it to deter any attempt at a hold-up. It was to be a temporary business – a one-off affair because the state gold shipment would no longer come through that area.

The wagon was so well built that the army had loaned Fort Carmin the use of one of their Gatling guns, to be mounted on the fully sealed wagon directly above the gold bars, which were stored safely underneath the strong, planked top. Everyone at the fort, and now the newly recruited civilians, were soon to learn that the Gatling was as much for show as any-thing else. The army Gatling guns were also used for show and to deter. The gun itself could only make sweeps of fire by manhandling the carriage from side to side by way of its two wheels. This was impracti-cal unless taking a full frontal assault, and the Indian Nations soon realized this. The loaned Gatling was to be removed from its two-wheeled gun carriage and mounted securely on the wagon, making an even greater load for the team of six horses to pull. However, to everyone at the fort it seemed a great deterrent.

'Left, wheel!' Morgan Philips, using his cavalry skills outside the fort on a large field, was not liked at all by the men who had been recruited from farms, sharecroppers and the like; they knew their own horses on which they sat, better than him. But the motley crew put up with his army bluster, shouted from under a black moustachioed lip, for the sake of five dollars a day and all they could eat.

Further down the field the heavy wagon, less the gold bullion, less the horses, less the Gatling gun, was positioned with a stake representing each of the team of six horses, so that the overall layout was a fair representation of what they were guarding. Philips positioned his six civilian outriders evenly, with Winchester rifles cradled in their laps, and then got them walking their horses round and round, so they felt at home with the work they were being paid to do. All seemed in order, all seemed well. Soon the 15 July would arrive.

***

Hoffman was pleased with the three men whom he had recruited on advice from Cactus Jim Bowry. They were to take the battle to the Gene Pinder gang of rogues from an area of tree cover that gave a reasonable view across the rocky terrain at the foot of the mesa. They had camped the night before in a little clearing off the gully that ran down the left side of the mesa. This gully was where Jack Hoffman had first ridden on the scouting trip around the mesa, with Cactus Jim riding the right-hand side of it.

The group entered the woodland just after dawn. It was about sixty yards away from the road where the heist would take place, at the rocky foot of the cliff. No fires were to be lit. They had good supplies of food, non-alcoholic drink and ammunition. Each man found a position to give best account of himself, knowing that three sharp-shooters were up a thousand feet to their right, ready to give much firing support at the evil gang. Buddy Cooper, Cactus Jim Bowry and Fred Kidman were in a good position, with their Sharps carbines loaded and pointing down from the cliff, awaiting the Pinder gang. Hoffmann insisted that all in the wood remain under cover until he gave the order to fire.

***

And so, an hour after dawn, the eight men led by Gene Pinder rode in a line past the wood, every one

147

of them looking around cautiously, each horse carrying saddle bags. At Pinder's side was Joshua Petersen, now de facto leader of the gang should Gene Pinder be killed. That false rep had won him much status. The plan was simple. Over the years Pinder had hatched an outrageous idea, where detail was of the utmost importance.

Gene Pinder had come from a rich family, but the money had been lost in bad investments by his father. Pinder, the youngest of four, had fallen into crime, and whilst in prison had befriended an old man who had attempted to steal gold bullion. Joe Bates had made a mess of the heist and was thrown in jail for what would be the rest of his life. Through his talking with Pinder he explained that a US gold bullion bar was of handy size, being about seven inches long. But it was the weight that was the problem for anyone who tried to steal it, as each bar weighed around twenty-seven pounds. In a bank vault they were stacked on heavy wooden cradles, eight bars wide by eight high. This Gene Pinder learned over many months of talking with his cell mate.

Over the months that turned into years, Pinder had time to brood: not only on how Fate had done him the dirty, but on how he could get his revenge on a world that didn't want him. Slowly the idea came that a strong horse could carry two bars of gold in a leather saddle bag, less than the weight of a fully grown man. This still left room for the rider to make a dash for it.

He stored the idea away in his mind, and as time passed Gene Pinder picked the mind of Joe Bates with the detailed skill of a mortician. He learned about the United States gold reserves, for Joe had worked for the Federal Reserve. How the American gold reserve worked to make the dollar a powerful, stable unit of currency, and also, most importantly, how he could learn when gold shipments would be made by the Union Pacific railroad. As the railroad spread across America, so the gold shipments would change. What had once been a strengthened wagon and a team of six horses to move the gold was fast dying out, at least for travelling long distances. The railroads were a much safer way of moving gold bullion. Again, this Gene Pinder stored to memory. He got out of prison eventually, found a job and a room to stay. But the idea of stealing gold and getting away with it filled his every moment. This was when he learned that the long run from Fort Carmin to Lusk by wagon would be the last one.

He had two years before this would happen. He had time to set up his plan and put it into action. Gene Pinder, still relatively young, joined up with his hoodlum friends of old and shared his plan for a gold heist that would beat all others and would succeed. Slowly the final part of Pinder's plan evolved. One man had a share-cropper shack ten miles from the road to Lusk. It would be a holding place where the gold could be stored temporarily if necessary, back-up that gave confidence to his ambitious plans.

Slowly and carefully Gene Pinder teased out his plan to seven bad men gathered around a table in his rented rooming house. He explained how two gold bars could be carried in a saddlebag, one bar on each side, and that the rider could still ride quickly in the normal way. Then he told them about the gold wagon journey that would go from Fort Carmin to Lusk. It would be the last one.

He then went on to explain how the gold would be stacked inside the strengthened wagon. This was the key to his plan, stealing it and getting away with the whole thing, because of the weight distribution required inside the wagon to stop it coming apart. Only two stacks of gold were possible, positioned fore and aft, eight bars wide by three bars high. He had even learned, and worked out, that this equalled two hundred and fifty thousand dollars. The trick was to take away the top layer of one stack only, so enough was left to indicate to the casual observer that nothing was amiss. The second trick was to find a way of removing the gold bars and transferring them to the saddle bags without letting anyone know. Slowly the last part of the plan evolved.

'The chances are,' growled Gene Pinder to the seven gathered around the table, amongst smoke and whiskey glasses, 'that a group of State troopers will accompany the wagon. They may use civilians led by an army man, because tying up troopers on a long ride could be costly. It doesn't matter which is used. I have found a place by scouting the area where we can hide men with Winchesters behind rocks and in gullies beneath the mesa that the Indians had before they were taken to reservations. The Lusk road runs right beneath it. Unfortunately, it is only about two miles down the road from the fort. But it doesn't matter, if my plan is kept to. There is enough hiding for all there. I want eight men to make this hidden ambush.

'My plan is for each man to cover the outriders or troopers, so they will see a Winchester pointed straight at them when our guys stand up suddenly. A shock that should keep them dumb, not to mention the wagon drivers. If only one shot got out, that could warn the fort, and that would spell disaster.' He looked around to an impressed silence, then went on to explain about the heavy weight of the gold bars.

'Each horse would have a good saddle bag on each side to carry one bar, because each bar weighs about twenty-seven pounds. No one is to be greedy, either, and we take only the top layer from the wagon. This is important,' Pinder insisted, 'and would still net us enough to buy a ranch each and have lots over.' Silence. Then came the questions.

'What about the troopers? They'll be witness to what we done. Yer gonna kill 'em all?'

'No. We'll tie 'em up and put them behind some rocks so they can't see what's going on. We all work quietly. There should be no noise anyway when removing the gold. When the first layer of gold bars has been put safely in our horses' saddle bags, one bar in each side, this won't take long, someone will shout out loudly, so's there's no mistaking it, that there's some riders a-coming. Then we all skedad-dle. When the troopers eventually get free we'll be far away with two bars of gold bullion safely on our horses. They'll look inside the open wagon top and see gold still there. Here's the clever thinking. There'll be two stacks of gold in the wagon, fore and aft. We'll only take the top layer from the front stack, the rear one will be part hidden by the wooden top. That is the usual way they build these special wag-ons for strength. With luck, they'll all decide to keep quiet. Why? They don't want to be shown up for not guarding the gold properly and could well ride on to Lusk because they'll think no gold is missing. If they don't, and go back to the fort for help, or for any other reason,' Pinder grinned widely, 'we'll still be miles away.'

FIFTEEN

As Hoffman lay with the three others in the wood, his Winchester prone and loaded, he felt a brooding silence across the whole area – it arrived even before the gang had ridden by the wood. It seemed as if Fate was waiting for them. As the gang took what looked like prearranged positions behind the detritus rocks and remnants from a long-past ice age, the gloom of what was about to be played out grew. Pinder knew the exact time almost to the minute when the gold wagon, and the six civilian escort riders, would leave the fort, due to a garrulous soldier in the fort who needed dollars in a hurry. Gene Pinder, who had worked on his plan for years whilst in prison, was on hair-trigger setting.

Soon the heavy wagon rolled into view with its six-man outriders. All the gang men were well hidden. Slowly they came into the heist area beneath the mesa cliff. Instantly all eight men rose, Winchesters at killing position, pointing directly at the six outriders, their leader, Morgan Philips, and two men high up on the jockey box controlling the team of six horses. Everyone froze as the horses were pulled up with loud cries of whoa. Silence reigned for some seconds as if the gang could not believe what they had achieved. Gene Pinder appeared on one side of the road leading out of the heist area, Joshua Petersen at the other side of the road.

'Now if everyone does exactly what they are told, no one gets hurt. You all understands?'

Pinder spoke, his harsh voice carried across the silence with power. 'All you outriders get off your horses, we will take care of them, allow us to tie you gentlemen up, for we are one of you, civilians. Please do as we say, and no harm will come to you.'

Hoffmann and the others watched as the outriders were tied up, tied together and led out of sight behind a series of rocks.

'OK! Let's begin,' shouted Pinder.

The jockey box was folded away on orders from Pinder, who seemed to know much, the operation revealed a substantial lid. Two gang members lifted the lid away to further reveal a compartment beneath which lay the gold. From his vantage point in the wood only sixty yards away, Jack Hoffmann could not make out what was going on. But from his position at the cliff top Fred Kidman could. He had brought the family's field glasses and was watching dumbfounded.

A gang member climbed up on to the wagon and removed a gold bar from the compartment. This was done with some difficulty due to the weight, but the bar was readily transferred to the saddle bag on one side of his own horse. Soon another bar was placed in the saddle bag on the other side. The outlaw, a grin on his bearded face, took back his Winchester – and so the process continued until a gun was fired into the air: Morgan Phillips had managed to partially free himself from the ropes, had reached his Winchester and fired it to call for help, then repositioned himself as a tied-up prisoner.

Gunfire was heard at the fort immediately. A lookout high up on his airy vantage point could see the stationary wagon and movement at the foot of the mesa two miles away. But it wasn't until he heard the gunshot that he ran down a flight of wooden steps, and seconds later, the captain of the guard knocked on the commander's door. Fourteen state troopers rode out through the opened gates of the fort in disciplined pairs, seven a side at a gallop.

Gene Pinder would have gone behind the rocks where the outriders lay tied up and shot them all, such was his rage. But there wasn't time, because for the plan to work, the gang had to transfer all sixteen gold bullion bars, weighing some twenty-seven pounds each, to the horses. And so they worked like demons.

Jack Hoffmann had seen the gold being transferred to the horses and marvelled at the gang's cleverness for such a stealing. He had heard the gunshot only too well. It was to warn the garrison at the fort. But this was still stealing by outlaws, and they would be happy to kill if things went wrong, of this he was sure. It steeled his will. He gave instructions to the other three men who were lying with rifles prone, to fire at will.

Winchester fire burst from the wood at the gang. 'Mind the outriders. Shoot as many outlaws as you can! But mind the outriders, who I think are now fighting back from behind the rock!' As the eight outlaws made for their horses, Jack Hoffmann shot two, Colin and Bill shot two more. Tommy missed and swore.

Immediately, a bad man who had seen approaching troopers appear around a bend, threw his rifle aside and leapt up on the wagon next to the Gatling gun. Morgan Philips, who had now fully escaped the ropes that held him and was helping his fellows, ran across to the wagon as the man began turning the firing handle to a bark from the first of six barrels. One after the other each barrel began firing in quick succession as the central shaft rotated.

At this point a great boom sounded from the top of the mesa, and the would-be gunner was blown from the wagon, a hole through the side of his chest the size of a fist. Buddy Cooper, a thousand feet up on the mesa, turned to Cactus Jim, the young man's face white. 'Never done killed a man 'afore. Had to stop him firing that thing, though.' Jim Bowry was as good with a six-gun as he was with the Sharps carbine in front of him, but he didn't know what to say to the boy and turned back to the fighting below. His careful aim took out an outlaw from his horse as he rode towards escape.

In that brief skirmish with the Gatling gun, a horse and trooper had been killed, but the remainder who pulled off the road were saved by its fixed position.

Two outriders who were now free from their ropes were mercilessly gunned down in the back by gang member Ricky Smith, a youth and probable psychopath, who had always wanted to kill someone, and now had.

Mayhem had now broken out. The firing continued from high up on the mesa, from the wood that hid Jack Hoffmann and his three accomplices, from remaining outriders who shot well from behind their rock cover, and the state troopers who had arrived and were joining the mêlée. Fred Kidman took careful aim with his Sharps at an outlaw who had shot one of the outriders and was carrying a bar of gold carefully to his horse, and the blast blew him away, blood covering the gold bar as he fell: it lay on the ground, a sort of metaphor for the whole business.

Eventually things went quiet, and a big man with a black, low-crown Stetson stepped out of the wood; he declared:

'I claim the bounty for stopping this heist on behalf of the citizenry of the town of Longhorn.' He turned to see a uniformed man riding a pure white horse arriving at the scene, and continued:

'If it hadn't been for this intervention by our citizens' posse, both up on that mesa and here in this wood cover, many more state troopers would have been killed – and this of course includes your civilian outriders.' The high-ranking solder on the white horse lifted his hand and shouted back across the distance, 'This request, with my blessing, will be put to the authorities in Washington. You have my word, sir.'

***

It was some time later that the full extent of the car-
nage was fully assessed. Both Gene Pinder and Joshua
Petersen, and another of the gang had gotten clean
away with their two bars of gold per man. Three
dodgers were nailed up in sheriffs' offices all over
the Territory. One by one the three were caught and
hung. Apart from Petersen's two, four gold bars were
never recovered.

***

Micky Dobson strode into the large timbered room
in his ranch house where the Longhorn town committee were gathered around his large polished
table. Everyone there was in some way kin folk to
the other: cousin, second cousin, brother and sister, some removed, some not actual family but
who fitted in well – the Harrises, the Dobsons, the
Kidmans, the Waterfords and the Davises, to mention a few.

'Well, Micky? Did that rider bring in the telegraph
message from Harpersville?'

'From Washington DC itself.' Dobson, now president of the committee, stood and looked at Marcus
Davis, who was kin to him twice removed, with a broad
smile on his face. He put the telegram on the table,
took a snort of his red eye, and read out the message
to everyone gathered there.

With reference to the attempted gold bullion robbery on the road between Fort Carmin and the
Lusk railhead, where it was to be transferred by the
Union Pacific Railroad to Washington DC, I, the
President of the Bank of the United States, hereby
authorise the payment of 25,000 dollars to the
Town's Committee of Longhorn, in the County of
Goodland, Wyoming Territory, in full recognition
of how this town's posse stopped the robbery. This
bounty payment is 10 per cent of the value of the
gold bullion. A copy of this testament is to be depos-
ited at the records office in Cheyenne, the capital
city of Wyoming Territory.

A cheer went up, hands were shaken, and much jol-
lity filled the room. Micky Dodson called for silence
and got it quickly.

'I would ask the posse to step forward. We were tele-
graphed before this telegram arrived and knew about
the amount of bounty reward, so a decision could be
made. Jack Hoffmann, the three sharp-shooters up
on the mesa cliff – Cactus Jim Bowry, Buddy Cooper
and Fred Kidman – and the three men who accompanied Mr Hoffmann in the wood at the bottom of the
mesa – Colin, Bill and Tommy – please stand.' They
all rose and stood.

'I have discussed this with the committee, without
some of you gentlemen present – apologies for that,
hope you understand our position over this – and
we have decided to award you all, irrespective of age
or experience, a large sum of money each from the

bounty, for your invaluable services. The remainder will be kept in our bank and owned by the town of Longhorn itself, to help it grow in the future. Money such as this, given freely to you seven gentlemen, will buy each of you a house or shop in Longhorn, a ranch outside perhaps and with money left over as well to set you up.' He looked at Buddy Cooper and smiled widely. 'You'll be able to buy your ma a nice house or ranch, Buddy, and take her away from Water Creek for good, if she so wishes.'

A loud cheer went up.

END